By the time Gray pulled the truck into the parking lot of the veterinary clinic, the dog had burrowed back against Aleja's chest.

She went to open the door, but Gray gripped her arm. "Wait. I'll come give you a hand down so you can keep her inside your coat."

"Such chivalry."

"Job of a firefighter. Opening doors for senior citizens and pregnant people."

"I'm not *that* pregnant yet. And I'm older than you, but not exactly retirement age."

"I know. I didn't mean—" He gritted his teeth. "Let me help you. We don't want the dog to get colder, and I don't want you to slip."

And she didn't want to come across as ungrateful after he'd gone out of his way to drive her here.

"Hey," she said when he got to her door and held out a hand to take her elbow. "I really appreciate the favor."

His cheeks were pink. Might have been from the wind, but his satisfied smile suggested not. "Glad I was the first to drive by."

She had to admit she was, too. There was something irresistible about the crisp scent coming off his jacket as she slid from the truck.

Dear Reader,

One of the best parts of writing the Sutter Creek series is the opportunity to explore the stories of characters who played small roles in previous books. Both the heroine and hero in *What to Expect When She's Expecting* had earlier cameos. Alejandra Brooks Flores first showed up as a contractor in *Their Nine-Month Surprise*, and Graydon Halloran entered the series with an appearance in *Snowbound with the Sheriff*. Their age difference and Alejandra's commitment to her job, her growing family and her friendship with Gray's sister complicate their journey from friends to forever—I hope you enjoy the ride!

What to Expect When She's Expecting starts a month after *Twelve Dates of Christmas* ends, and anyone eagle-eyed might remember Aleja wasn't feeling too well at the end of December. Being pregnant with twins will do that to a person! Throw in an adorable German wirehaired pointer puppy, and Aleja and Gray have the perfect blueprint for a family—provided she's willing to alter her original plans. Luckily, firefighting has taught Graydon to be a patient, persistent man, and he's willing to do what it takes to win the heart of the woman he's loved for decades.

Keep up-to-date on new Sutter Creek books and exclusive extras by visiting my website, www.laurelgreer.com, where you'll find the latest news and a link to sign up for my newsletter. I'd love to hear your thoughts on Alejandra and Graydon's story— come say hello on Facebook, Instagram or TikTok. I'm @laurelgreerauthor on all three.

Happy reading!

Laurel

What to Expect When She's Expecting

—

LAUREL GREER

HARLEQUIN

SPECIAL
EDITION

Recycling programs
for this product may
not exist in your area.

ISBN-13: 978-1-335-72405-2

What to Expect When She's Expecting

Copyright © 2022 by Lindsay Macgowan

For questions and comments about the quality of this book, please contact us at CustomerService@Harlequin.com.

Harlequin Enterprises ULC
22 Adelaide St. West, 41st Floor
Toronto, Ontario M5H 4E3, Canada
www.Harlequin.com

Printed in U.S.A.

Raised in a small town on Vancouver Island, **Laurel Greer** grew up skiing and boating by day and reading romances under the covers by flashlight at night. Ever committed to the proper placement of the Canadian *eh*, she loves to write books with snapping sexual tension and second chances. She lives outside Vancouver with her law-talking husband and two daughters. At least half her diet is made up of tea. Find her at www.laurelgreer.com.

Books by Laurel Greer

Harlequin Special Edition

Sutter Creek, Montana

From Exes to Expecting
A Father for Her Child
Holiday by Candlelight
Their Nine-Month Surprise
In Service of Love
Snowbound with the Sheriff
Twelve Dates of Christmas
What to Expect When She's Expecting

Visit the Author Profile page at Harlequin.com.

For Sadie, who would much rather have
a Penny of her own than a book dedication.

Chapter One

The luggage cart groaned in protest as Gray Halloran slung another box onto the rickety platform. The cart would have to put up with the abuse. Lunch at the soon-to-be rebranded Moosehorn River Lodge started in fifteen minutes, and Gray had promised his sister he'd get his truckload of stuff up the elevator and into his room before any of her paying guests sat down to eat.

Having to move to her property was embarrassing enough without also inconveniencing her business.

His cell buzzed with a text.

Emma: You're just unloading now?

The anxious knot in his stomach tightened. Spying on me? he typed.

I can see the parking lot from my office. You should have been here an hour ago.

He sighed. She wasn't wrong. Sorry. Mom conscripted me when I dropped off the stuff I'm storing at the ranch. Had to fix a busted barn gate. I'll hurry.

Please do. Get in by 11.

He eyed the neatly stacked cart, searching for any extra space. Three years of working for Sutter Creek Fire and Rescue in his small Montana hometown had made him an expert at rolling hose and packing first-aid equipment with precision. Organizing clothes and books was a cinch, along with the minimal number of personal items he'd brought with him. He'd bring over anything else he needed another day, after he figured out what was necessary and what he could leave at the ranch until he found an ideal living arrangement.

Essentially, anything he could afford on his firefighter's salary that didn't require him to mooch off family. But given the impossible state of the rental market in Sutter Creek mid–ski season, he couldn't be picky. Working on Emma's maintenance crew on his days off would make up the difference between what he could swing in rent and the rack rate on a lodge suite. Would mean he could live with himself, too.

I'll put you up, Gray. Everyone needs a hand when they're starting out.

Kind words. Had he not been attuned to it, he might have missed his sister's couched pity. His family loved to see him as a kid instead of a twenty-five-year-old man who got paid to save lives and property.

Damn it, the cart was bursting. He'd have to come back for a second load. He locked up his truck then pushed the cart along the path, glad for whichever employee had scraped last night's snowfall from the concrete.

Tomorrow, that employee would probably be him.

Despite kicking himself for being late, he couldn't help but enjoy the morning sun warming the winding path. It was the first blue sky in a few days, and he loved not having wind biting at his face for a change. Also, to be wearing jeans, work boots and a jacket rather than turnout gear.

The fresh snowfall draped like a quilt over native-plant gardens and pathways. Marshmallow-fluff accumulations covered the tin roof's hodgepodge of peaks. His great-grandfather built this place back before power tools were a thing, which always blew his mind. The lodge, with its log sides and green roof marrying with the trees on all sides, had a way of making even Gray feel small. Tough to do—he was on the tall side of six-three.

He was almost to the rustic entrance when a streak of beige canvas darted across his path and behind one of the thick pillars.

He halted, jerking the load. Something on the cart snapped and the base tilted. His boxes shifted, tilting precariously. He lurched toward them, destabilizing the cart even more.

A box tumbled to the ground. Then another.

Thud. Thud.

One more.

Thunk.

He caught a fourth, but missed a fifth, which landed with a crash. *Crud.* Probably his plates. Neck hot with annoyance, he gripped the heavy box and used his hip to brace the rest of the stack.

"Oh, no!" A feminine voice came from over his shoulder.

He glanced back as a familiar face peeked around the wide post serving as a hiding spot.

Alejandra Brooks Flores's doe-brown eyes widened, her plush lips forming a horrified O. Her light brown complexion was washed out. Almost green around the edges.

"Are you okay?" he said.

She was still the most gorgeous woman he'd ever seen. So much for being over his crush on his childhood neighbor—the one who happened to be over a decade older than him and was joined at the hip with his oldest sister, Nora.

She shifted around the post, tilting her head at the lopsided cart. Taking the front support bar in her hands, she pushed the cart back to straight. "I'm so sorry, Gray. I didn't mean to get in your way. I think you've lost the front wheel."

No doubt that was the problem.

Of more concern? He'd lost his heart to this

woman when he was a teenager and had never managed to get over her.

Carpenter's overalls hugged the curves he'd been mapping in his head since he was old enough to know that gazing at a woman was one of the better pleasures life had to offer. A tool belt hugged her lush hips. She'd tucked a pencil behind her ear, amongst the little curls escaping from a thick, dark brown braid. Clear eye protection perched on the top of her head.

Alejandra Brooks Flores and her safety attire. Irresistible.

But not only did their eleven-year age difference prevent her from seeing him as anything but her best friend's little brother, pursuing her would mean endless grief from his three sisters and older cousin Jack. No thanks.

So, as always, he'd hide his feelings and hope she never noticed the emoji-worthy hearts in his eyes.

Clearing his throat and attempting to clear what he knew was a lovesick look off his face, he put down his box and righted the fallen carton. He stacked them to the side of the portico in case a guest came by. Emma would no doubt tsk and fuss that he'd cluttered the otherwise pristine entryway. "I told Emma this cart was on its last legs, but she insisted it was in working order."

Aleja winced. "And then I had to run in front of it and test its limits."

"You couldn't have known." With the somewhat

smushed boxes in a tidy pile by a barrel filled with winter kale, he started to unload the remainder.

"What's in the boxes?"

"All my earthly belongings. My apartment building got sold and is getting torn down," he said. "What am I saying—you'd know that. Did your dad bid on the contract for the rebuild?"

She shook her head. "Timing wasn't right. But I do know the project."

"Yeah, they gave us two months' notice, but nothing showed up in my price range, not with it being high season. I promised everything but my first-born child to Emma in exchange for a lodge room."

"You didn't want to move to Bozeman?"

"Too far a commute."

Aleja's throat bobbed, as if she was trying not to gag.

"You still dealing with the flu you had back before Christmas?"

"No, I'm all better."

It didn't look like it, but she didn't offer up more of an explanation, so he went back for another box. "Emma and I are swapping labor for one of the loft rooms. Means I feel like less of a freeloader."

Her eyebrows lifted. "Huh. Wouldn't have thought you'd want to tie up your time."

"I'll make it work." Did she underestimate him like his family did? Then again, she was probably the recipient of Nora's complaints whenever Gray had to skip out on ranch work because of his rotations and training. Nora assumed that because she loved their ranch more than anything, her younger siblings should, too. He had other priorities—like saving lives.

He studied the pile he'd made. "I'll have to find a dolly to get these upstairs. Or maybe there's another luggage cart."

"I have a dolly," Aleja offered, hands still braced to keep the cart level.

"Thanks. Might need to take you up on that. I take it the reno is in full swing?" He hadn't realized Aleja was working the lodge overhaul. Last he'd heard, she'd been contracted to build a mansion on the other side of Moosehorn Lake for some Silicon Valley billionaire.

"We're on track so far." She turned a shade greener than before.

"Are you *sure* you're okay?"

"A hundred percent."

If she said so. But his EMT training didn't like the sheen of sweat dotting her forehead. "I saw the plans in my sister's office. Your dad did a wicked job. Artsier than some of his usual stuff. I love the romance-in-the-woods vibe."

Her cheek flinched. "My dad didn't design this project. I did. I'm in charge."

His throat dried up. "Of the whole thing?"

She drew up to her full five feet eight inches. Barely above his chin but sporting a glare that in no uncertain terms guaranteed she could take him to the ground if she put her mind to it.

That possibility was far too intriguing.

"Problem with that?" she asked.

Yes. Only because I want to kiss you.

"Of course not," he said. "I'm sorry I made assumptions. I thought you were working on a new mansion for some out-of-towner."

"It fell through." She pressed her lips together. "I can handle the management of this project, Graydon."

"I know, I—"

"Some guys give me attitude, but I didn't expect it from you. You grew up with your mom and Nora running your family's spread. They'd ream you out for days if they heard you questioning a woman's capacity to lead in a trades profession."

His cheeks flamed hot. She was right. "You must know I think you do good work."

"Then why'd you ask me if I was running 'the whole thing'?"

He jammed his hands into his jacket pockets. "I—uh—I meant I was surprised to see you. Not because I don't think you *can* do the job. I didn't know *that* you were doing the job—"

"You said it like it was a problem," she said.

"Aleja…" He forced a blank expression.

"Is it a problem?"

"Of course not." This clearly wasn't the first time she'd had this argument. He wished he hadn't misspoken and come across as one more prick determined to undervalue her.

"Your sister trusts me. And I don't want you in her ear, trying to change her mind."

"I wouldn't do that. I'm glad you got the contract."

He swallowed, trying to get the moisture back in his mouth. Aleja, here. Daily. *Damn.*

There was no chance of an apartment he could afford turning up in town until May at the earliest. Until the seasonal mountain workers left town, he'd be living in the lodge.

Running into Aleja all the time.

Four months of having to ignore how beautiful she was in overalls and a tool belt.

Yikes.

Back in ninth grade, his friends had worshipped Katy Perry and Rihanna. He'd had Alejandra Brooks Flores coming in on careers day to talk about women in trades, all competence and kindness, with an extra smile for him and a chat about how she'd heard he'd played well in his last hockey game.

His feelings had gotten easier to hide when he went to college and then came home to join the department. His siblings hadn't teased him about being infatuated with Aleja since before he was with his college girlfriend, and he intended to keep it that way.

Not by making himself scarce, though. He'd committed to putting in hours for his sister. Flaking out on Emma wasn't an option, not if he wanted to shed the spoiled-youngest-child albatross he'd hung around his own neck as a teenager. Years of being responsible hadn't freed him from that reputation, but he had to believe he'd eventually succeed.

He took the last box off the cart and added it to his pile.

Relief shot across Aleja's face, and she dropped the edge of the cart.

"Oh, crap—" She slapped a hand across her mouth and took off, darting out from under the portico, down the gravel path to the river, until she was out of sight.

Gray stared at the corner of the building where she disappeared. His gut nagged him. The boxes would have to wait.

He pushed the broken cart to the side, pulled out his phone and found his text thread with Emma.

He winced at her last message—get in by 11—and checked his watch: 10:55.

Sorry, Em.

He typed his reply.

2 probs. (1) Your cart is garbage. (2) Aleja is sick & might need 1st aid. Sorry re: pile @ front. Will move ASAP.

Knowing he'd get an earful regardless, he took off down the same path as Aleja.

Alejandra rested her forehead against the log side of the lodge. The winter-chilled wood cooled her clammy skin. So much for finding a garbage can— she'd settled for the ground next to an unsuspecting rhododendron.

She took a deep breath. *All right, stomach. I get it. Toast is the most offensive food known to humanity.*

Maybe now she'd feel less queasy for the rest of the day.

Unlikely. The morning sickness she'd been lucky enough to be dealing with since week freaking four of her pregnancy was more like all-day nausea. It had been going on for five weeks and was not abating.

And to have Gray Halloran witness her sprint for privacy? Embarrassment flooded in, twisting her empty stomach. The man wasn't known for being a vault—her best friend Nora had complained about Gray's loose lips a million times when he was younger. What if he figured out the reason for her nausea and told his sister? She wanted to get established on the project before Emma or her work crew found out she was expecting.

At least her overalls hid her bloated belly. Most of her pants were way too tight despite her meagre diet of crackers, toast and her abuela's corn tortillas.

Pregnancy was a hundred percent awful so far.

And she could not be more excited to be miserable.

Life was nothing if not full of chaos energy, and right after spending Christmas hiding how sick she was, Aleja had got a call from Emma saying she needed a contractor. On the heels of the lake mansion getting scrapped and used to grappling for contracts in the small Montana ski town where she'd grown up, she wasn't going to let being pregnant get in the way of a career-changing opportunity.

Emma had big dreams of turning Moosehorn River Lodge into a five-star wedding destination. Aleja intended to facilitate them.

She was starting the overhaul downstairs, transforming the honeycomb of storage rooms and old staff housing into a larger multipurpose area. When construction shifted to the grand dining hall in a couple of months, Emma would have an alternate place to serve meals to her guests. Aleja couldn't wait to get started on turning the lodge basement into a cozy nook for dining and lounging.

Frustratingly, until she could trust her stomach, she was better off in the fresh air.

She leaned back against the log wall. *End game, Aleja—a baby. And all that joy.*

She'd been desperate to be a mom ever since her first nephew was born when she was barely twenty. Her Tía Aleja role—*Ti-leja*, in toddler-speak—had only satisfied for so long, though. She had no problem being a "come from a big family, want a big family" cliché. It should have happened with her ex. Thank God she'd found out he was a liar before they'd gotten married. After breaking things off with Trace, she'd worried she was never going to find the right partner. But then her youngest sister and her wife went the donor route and ended up with Aleja's beautiful niece, and she'd been inspired to rely on science instead of an unreliable man. Two rounds of IUI later, and she got two blue lines.

She splayed a hand on her belly and took a breath of cold mountain air. *Yup.* She and the sprout were going to be fine as a duo, especially surrounded by Aleja's parents, abuela, siblings and their own families.

"You're going to be loved, kiddo. More than you can handle. I promise."

Of course, she'd been throwing promises around like snowballs in a schoolyard these past few weeks. She was going to have to work faster than she ever had in her life if she wanted to get this project done before her baby arrived.

That meant efficiency, every day.

Not needing twenty-minute breaks to retch in the bushes.

"Aleja?" Gray's low voice drifted from around the corner.

Oh, crud, he'd followed her. Maybe if she stayed quiet…

His footsteps slowed and his big frame came into view. "There you are."

He'd been taller than her since he was in elementary school but looking up at him was always a bit of a trip. A baseball cap covered his messy blond hair. Gold stubble glinted on his usually clean-shaven face, and his chest was broad enough to sub in for one of the weight-bearing walls they'd need to replace as they tore out the existing studs.

The universe had not skipped any steps when forming the firefighter's square jaw and tilted smile.

Objectively, she could accept he was attractive. *Subjectively*, not so much.

He was her best friend's little brother.

Since when had she started noticing he was muscular and tall and saved lives for a living and in no way could be described as "little" anymore? Was it pregnancy hormones? *Argh.*

Her cheeks heated, prickling from the January nip in the air. She put on her best nothing-to-see-here expression. "Did you need something else?"

He cocked a brow and handed her a bottle of water. "Yeah, to figure out if you need medical help."

"Absolutely not."

"You were sick, though."

"It happens." She took a few small sips and rinsed her mouth before straightening away from the wall. Time to get to work.

Sliding the plastic bottle into her jacket pocket, she unclipped her respirator from her tool belt and shifted past him.

His gaze caught on the protective equipment. "Those are heavy duty filters."

She turned to face him. "And?"

"Thought my sister said everything was tested for lead and asbestos."

Her stomach jittered. He was too observant. He was also treading close to questioning her expertise, which wasn't going to fly. As a woman in the trades, Latinx to boot, she'd been second-guessed her whole career. She sure as hell wasn't going to take it from the kid who'd pretended to be a poltergeist on the nights she and Nora had slept in the hayloft of th Hallorans' barn.

"Correct—the site is lead-free, and we kn

where any asbestos is and have a removal crew lined up," she said.

"But the filters—"

"I just need to be careful," she said. "Long story."

His eyebrows furrowed.

Acid burned her throat. She covered her mouth with a fist and looked away.

Come on, stomach. Hold off the revolt.

At least until she got rid of Gray and made sure the sledgehammers were swinging.

He studied her with an EMT's eye. "Do you need to sit down?"

"No, I need to get to—" Nope. The miniscule amount of water she'd consumed was losing its fight for internal supremacy. Whirling back to the rhodo, she tried to hide as much as she could.

Gray swore and came closer, resting a palm on her back and rubbing a soothing circle.

She hunched over, trying to regain control over her body.

"What's going on, Aleja?"

Son of a mother, for all she felt like garbage baking in the sun, Gray's hand, steady and comforting, was exactly what she needed.

No way was she going to try swallowing anything, but she couldn't handle the taste in her mouth. She rinsed her mouth out. "Nothing you need to be concerned about."

"I disagree," he said. "If you've got food poisoning or a virus, you shouldn't be here."

"I'm fine."

"You're not. You should be snuggled on your couch with tea and Netflix."

"I don't have time to rest. This job needs to be done by July." She straightened. The too-quick motion set her head spinning. She wobbled.

He steadied her shoulders with both hands. "One day won't—"

"You have a pile of boxes jamming up your sister's main entrance. You should go deal with them."

"I can't leave you if you're shaky. If it's not flu, what is it? Prolonged nausea—" His eyes widened, flicking down to her stomach. He swiped a palm over his mouth. "Oh. *Oh.* Are you preg— Uh, never mind. Not my business."

Oh, crap. Gray had outstanding *heavy respirator* plus *puking* plus *dizziness* math.

"Y-you know," she stammered, "the only time it's appropriate to assume a person is pregnant is when a baby is literally emerging from their body."

He laughed awkwardly. "Had that happen to me on my second week on the job. I showed up at what I thought was a fender bender and discovered Missy Flanagan—crowning—instead. Turned out she wasn't able to teach a full day's kindergarten while in labor and still get to the hospital in time."

"I'll make sure to call the firehouse if I can't make it to the hospital," she said.

"Call 911, but yeah, that's what we get paid for."

"Gray…" This was delicate—if news got out, would her team trust her ability to lead and do the work? "I have a couple of old-school workers and subcontractors, and if any of them have an outdated picture in their heads of what a pregnant woman can and can't do, I'll be screwed. I'm going to tell them soon, but until I find the right time, please don't say anything to anyone, including Emma. Only my family and Nora know."

He palmed the top of his ball cap. "You think I'd talk behind your back?"

"I can't take the risk of not being clear." Her first ultrasound appointment on Thursday, delayed by a week due to a scheduling error, would bring some relief. But she'd still only be nine weeks along and vulnerable to miscarriage. Twelve weeks seemed safer. "Can't you see why I need to be cautious?"

A shadow crossed his face. Disappointment?

"Your secret's safe," he said after a long pause. "You take care of yourself."

He strode off, shoulders stiff and frown firmly in place.

She groaned. He'd connected the dots. What a slippery slope.

And an even slipperier slope? Watching him walk away and seeing nothing but a whole lot of man under all that denim and flannel.

Chapter Two

Some days, Gray walked away from his shifts as a firefighter feeling like he could take on the world, not just his quiet life in small-town Montana.

And then there were days like today, where he had to caffeinate like a college student pulling an all-nighter in order to make it home safely. An extra-large pity serving of coffee steamed away in his console, comped by the owner of Sweets and Treats after hearing about how busy B shift had been. Next to it, the ginger tea he'd spontaneously picked up and now needed to figure out how to deliver to Aleja without looking like a tool.

The bakery owner hadn't asked who the tea was for, though she'd shot him a curious look. Aside from the bulk order he put in when it was his turn to buy coffee for his coworkers, he rarely ordered anything except his triple-shot Americano.

It wasn't easy disguising interest in a woman living in a town where most year-round residents had known him since he was in diapers. But if he wanted to keep from becoming coffee-klatch gossip, he needed to stay subtle.

Tea is not subtle.

Neither was his concern for her, though.

He gripped his steering wheel and blasted cold air on his face, easing his truck around the slippery turns leading to the lake.

Was Aleja feeling sick every morning, or had the nausea he'd witnessed two days ago been a onetime thing?

Not his business. She'd made that clear. And it wasn't like he didn't have a hundred other things to focus on.

He'd only managed three hours of sleep over his twenty-four-hour shift because a couple of genius tourists had decided it was safe to ice climb in the blizzard that covered the county yesterday. His crew had been called to support the search and rescue team. They'd barely gotten a break before a structure fire had occupied the rest of their night. Never fun at the best of times, but worse with ice crystals pelting his face and hose connections freezing up.

While in the blazing house, he'd been sharp as usual, but after he emerged, he hadn't been able to rid himself of the image of the broken crib he'd happened upon while searching for residents. Blessedly empty—the house was long abandoned, the fire likely started by an arsonist.

The minute he'd sat his ass down in the truck on the ride back to the station, those images had shifted to Aleja. *Pregnant* Aleja. Aleja, about to be a mother with her own nursery.

He had a million questions, starting with *who's the father*, and *how did he get so lucky?*

He hadn't realized she was involved with someone. Or maybe she'd gotten back together with her ex? No matter the identity of the father, Gray's infinitesimal chance of catching her attention had just incinerated.

His feelings weren't going to burn up as quickly as his chances, though. Nor was his concern.

If she saw him bringing her tea as weird, he'd blame it on sleep deprivation.

He'd drop it off, feigning some casual concern, before starting his maintenance shift with Emma's fiancé, Luke, whose family owned the other half of the lodge. The guy was also the local wildlife warden. How he matched with Gray's indoorsy sister, Gray didn't know, but the pair seemed deliriously happy.

A few minutes later, his sister's name popped up as an incoming call.

He groaned and pressed the answer button on his steering wheel. "I'm late."

"Yeah, I can tell, given you're not at the lodge yet. Hate to nag you, but I need you, pronto." Her voice rang over his truck's navigation system. "Luke's out dealing with a fish hatchery problem, and no way am

I letting Hank up on a ladder to deal with the icicles. I don't like having half the building surrounded by caution tape. If you're going to commit to shifts, I need you here when you say you'll be here. I have a schedule to keep to. Otherwise, I spend the day dealing with guest complaints about the stack of boxes in the entrance during check-in time."

He was never going to live that one down. "I understand your schedule is important. But house fires need to be put out." He stopped himself before he added *and nauseated women need to be checked on.* Aleja wouldn't appreciate him sharing her morning sickness with his sister, even if it might have earned him a pass on having clogged up the portico. "I'm on my way, Em, but we got back to the station late, and the roads are slick."

"I heard about the fire." Her tone gentled. "Mom was worried."

"It was nothing unusual."

"You know Mom. She'd prefer you be riding horses alongside Nora rather than a fire engine."

"No one freaks out when Jack parachutes into the middle of a raging inferno." He scowled at the road ahead. His family should have been well used to firefighting emergencies by now. Gray's cousin Jack, who'd been raised alongside the four Halloran siblings since childhood, was a smokejumper out in Oregon.

"You're her baby," Emma said. "She always worries about you more."

"Yeah, I know." At least it meant she cared.

"I'll be there in fifteen." Gray blew out a breath. "Right after I drop something off with Aleja."

"Huh?" He could almost hear Emma scowl when she said, "You're not getting in her way, are you? I don't want the crew to deal with unnecessary interruptions. This renovation is stretching everything Luke, Hank and I have."

Gray chafed at the perception he didn't understand basic social conduct. He'd consciously worked to get his spoiled head out of his ass after college—getting better at keeping confidences and doing what he could to help at the ranch when it didn't conflict with firefighting or the paramedic training he was picking away at. He *did* understand the renovation on what had been the Emerson Wilderness Lodge was a hell of a risk for Emma, her fiancé and her grandfather-in-law-to-be.

"It'll only take a minute."

"Just deal with the icicles as fast as you can, okay?" Emma said.

"I will, I will."

He finished mainlining his coffee and parked his truck in his designated spot around the back of the building.

Nerves jittering over the likelihood of making a fool of himself, he stopped in his room to change out of his uniform before heading for the basement. The staircases were closed off to prevent guest access and to keep out dust and noise, so he went out the back way from the loft down to the dining room

and then took the stairs off the wide balcony over-
looking the river.

Morning sun glittered off the water, promising a
pretty day. Frigid air nipped his nose. He'd been so
focused on remembering to bring the tea, he hadn't
thought to throw on a jacket.

Temporary tents lined the water side of the lodge,
full of carpentry equipment but empty of people,
minus a pale twentysomething guy sitting on a stool,
wearing a ball cap with Security printed on it. Unfa-
miliar. Maybe one of the seasonal employees picking
up some extra work.

Gray nodded a greeting, gripped the tea in one
hand and hitched a thumb at the building with the
other. "Is the boss inside?"

The security guard pointed at the closed door.
"Through there."

Here goes nothing.

He entered through a weatherworn wooden door.
Voices rang out from the end of the short hallway.
The passage opened into a large room where a six-
person crew encircled a sheet of plywood resting on
two sawhorses.

Aleja was explaining something on a diagram
to them. She straightened as he approached. "Need
something, Gray?"

Crap, he had not expected to catch the attention
of all her workers.

"I, uh, have a question for you. I can wait."

Brows narrowed, she nodded. "Give me a second."

Damn it. He should not have done this. Not only

did she seem confused as anything by his presence, but she also appeared steadier than she had two mornings ago.

He waited on the edge of the torn-up room. Two minutes later, she sent everyone to get back to demolition.

Not needing witnesses, he backed into the hall. His pulse thrummed in his ears, competing with the sledgehammers the crew were driving into the walls.

She rounded the corner, studying him like she still didn't know what to make of his presence.

"I just got off my shift," he explained weakly.

"Okay…"

"What I mean is, I would have come to see if you were feeling better yesterday, but I was at the station."

"You don't need to check on me. I'm healthy," she said.

"I know. And that's great." Had she been expecting the pregnancy? Accidents happened. He wouldn't be here, otherwise. Hopefully if it was a surprise, it was one she wanted.

Not knowing what to say, he thrust the drink at her. "In case you're feeling queasy this morning. When my crewmate was pregnant last year, she swore by the stuff."

She took the cup and sniffed the small opening. "Oh, ginger. How thoughtful." Her cheeks, which had been too pale the last time he saw her, turned rosy bronze. "It's also… I don't want my employees and subcontractors asking too many questions,

Gray. Bringing me tea is sweet, but it's the kind of gesture people notice."

He balled his fists to keep from rubbing one of her shoulders, or even brushing a hand across her cheek. She looked like she needed reassurance, and his instincts leaned toward touching the people he loved.

It's not love. It never was.

Or so he'd keep trying to convince himself.

"Like I mentioned, I won't say anything," he assured her.

A dark eyebrow arched. "Similar to how well you promised not to tell your hockey coach Nora was interested in him, but did anyway? Or telling your mom when Jack's college girlfriend got pregnant?"

Oh, good grief. "I was a teenager, Aleja. You can't seriously be using that as the yardstick."

She looked a little sheepish. "I guess I've hung on to a picture of you as younger than you are."

His heart sank. Good thing he'd never tried to broach the subject of romantic feelings—his *or* hers. Talk about avoiding nuclear levels of awkwardness. At least through staying silent, he was preserving their friendship.

"You're not the only one who's still in that habit," he said.

When he was fifteen, he'd found out his parents had lied to him every time they'd assured him they'd planned to have him. He'd taken a while to figure out where he really fit in his family. Lashed out at his sisters' and Jack's teasing about him being an accident. None of them had made good choices at the time.

He learned his lesson then—bury his feelings deep, and no one would be able to use them against him.

Hence no one knowing he'd kept admiring Aleja from afar long after his family thought he'd gotten over his teenage crush.

He'd better scoot before his sister came poking around and started connecting the dots.

"Enjoy the tea," he said. "I better go—I have some icicles to knock down."

"Be careful."

The hint of worry in her tone kept him wondering the entire time he was up on the scissor lift.

A few hours after Gray brought her tea, Aleja still hadn't managed to finish it. Setting the paper cup down on the table in the nook off the lodge's dining room, she spread out a series of sketches.

She needed to hammer down Emma's wishes before putting through a massive custom-materials order.

She'd never had such a strong visual of how she wanted a renovation to turn out. The dining area, especially, with its soaring ceilings. She could almost smell the stain she'd use on a new loft railing and the grout for repairing the river-rock fireplace.

Emma joined her a minute later, carrying two mugs. She sat, plunking one in front of Aleja. Her crisp navy suit and white blouse clashed against the lurid floral of the couch. Only her long brown ponytail fit in with the rustic environment.

"Help yourself to the coffee," Emma said. "I'm

desperate for a pick-me-up. Luke got called out at the crack of misery and I didn't get back to sleep."

"No, thank you." Aleja lifted her reheated tea. "I'm set."

Emma sniffed the air. "Mmm, smells like ginger. Chai?"

Aleja shrugged in response. It was way safer to be vague.

Emma pushed up her purple-framed glasses and studied the sketches. "Ooh, Luke's going to love this. It'll be like walking into a forest. A classy, pristine forest."

A grin pushed past Aleja's nerves. "Exactly what I was going for. But it's not going to be cheap. I want to be certain before I start placing orders for all the specialty wood. The branches I need in place of spindles come from a company in North Carolina."

"Nowhere local has something similar?"

"Not that'll meet safety requirements."

A flash of jeans-clad legs caught her eye through the tall, angled windows of the dining room. Gray was out on the balcony, scaling a ladder.

Emma glanced in the direction of Aleja's gaze. "Oh, good, he's almost done."

He was up so high.

Aleja's mouth dried out.

Silly, really. She climbed ladders daily, and by the looks of those muscled thighs, he was more than stable.

Her heart still skipped.

Maybe it's not the height.

"Aleja? You aren't worried, are you? Gray's hopeless with a lot of stuff, but if he can climb a ladder to fight a fire, I'm sure he's fine out on my deck."

Aleja's cheeks were too warm. Probably pink, too. Shoot. She snapped her attention back to the meeting. "Yeah, just, uh, thinking about the safety equipment the drywallers and painters are going to need."

"Whatever it takes. Having cream walls is going to be so much better than the cedar panels. I need the neutral backdrop for wedding decor."

"And you're sure you want the railings, staircases and beams to be distinctive?" She pointed a pencil at the sketches of her plan to pull the outside indoors. Branches twisting into railing panels to give the impression of staring through a tree canopy. Posts with intact bark. Halved logs for stair runners.

So long as she could transform the place before her belly grew too round for her to rip up the olive green monstrosity of a carpet and lay wood flooring, this lodge could fuel her business for the next ten years.

As her dad got closer to retirement, she needed to distinguish herself from his practical, straightforward work. That, plus her August due date, plus figuring out how to keep her crew's confidence once they found out she was pregnant meant a precarious balance, but she'd manage it.

It would be good practice for balancing parenting and work after the babies were born. She wasn't going to compromise on the quality of her projects, but she intended to prioritize family, as her parents had done. Lots of time for couch snuggles and deep discussions. Time exploring the plains of their property and the mountains surrounding the spread. Getting stuffed with sopes and her abuela's playlists of George Jones and Consuelo Velázquez—*we're deep diving beyond "Bésame Mucho," mija*—with ideas and humor and love. Always love.

Her phone buzzed on the table next to the sketches. Speaking of Abuela. Aleja swore she had a sixth sense for knowing when someone was thinking of her.

"My grandmother," she said to Emma. "I'll call her back."

"Gosh, don't worry about it. Take the call."

She grabbed her cell and walked the few yards to the window, then answered. "Abuela, hi."

"Ah, tú contestaste."

"Yes, I answered, but I only have a minute." She often conversed in Spanish with Abuela, but she didn't speak it as fluently as English. Thinking about vocabulary and conjugations slowed her down, and this phone call needed to be quick. "I'm in a meeting, and I'm planning to work late tonight to make up for tomorrow morning."

Movement by the eaves caught her eye. She tried to peer up at Gray without Emma noticing she was watching him. He wielded the roof rake competently. Lord, she appreciated a man who knew his way around tools—

Except when he's Nora's brother.

"Don't wear yourself out, Alejita. The first trimester is hard."

"You don't say," she said lightly.

"Which is why I called—I want to come to your appointment with you tomorrow."

Aleja huffed out a laugh. "Being alone is kind of the name of the game, Abuela. I knew it going in."

"As long as I'm around, you never have to be alone. Please, I'd love to be there. You're going to rob me of the first glance at my great-grandchild? I take my bisabuela duties seriously. Your precious one could be the last one I meet."

"Twist the knife, why don't you?" Aleja couldn't help watching as Gray descended the ladder. Those jeans were worn in all the right places, leaving nothing to the imagination. Wow. Whoever took Graydon Halloran to bed at night was damn lucky.

He reached the deck and glanced through the window. His gaze landed on her. His mouth spread in a slow grin.

Oh, no. Had he caught her staring? Awareness scalded her cheeks. She looked away, refocusing on her grandmother's absurd suggestion she wasn't going to be around much longer.

"Abuela, you're not going anywhere soon."

"Except to Bozeman with you tomorrow?"

No one was more persistent than Adelita Brooks when she had an idea in her head. Without her example, Aleja wouldn't be where she was today—running a business with her dad and expecting the baby who would complete her little family.

She also knew when it was time to give in. "I'll pick you up at eight. The appointment is at nine. Also, I need to go by the building supply store after."

"Deal."

After saying goodbye, Aleja returned to Emma, who was doing a terrible job of pretending she hadn't been listening in.

"Is your grandmother okay?" Emma asked.

"Fit as a fiddle."

"You're sure?" The tips of Emma's ears grew pink. "I wasn't meaning to eavesdrop, but I couldn't help but hear you tell her she wasn't going anywhere. And that she has an appointment."

Aleja fidgeted with the cuff of the long sleeve of her T-shirt. "It's nothing to worry about."

Emma's forehead creased.

Uh-oh. If Emma remained unconvinced, she'd probably start asking around about Abuela's health, which would start all sorts of rumors.

Unless she filled Emma in on her own truth.

Tomorrow. After her ultrasound, provided everything went well, she'd talk to Emma about her tiny, massive surprise.

Chapter Three

Gray rounded the lodge's outside path after dinner that night, whistling to himself. Aleja had been watching him when he was up the ladder—knowledge a guy could feed off for weeks.

It didn't mean anything. She's obviously involved with someone else.

He was heading for the balcony stairs when a sharp curse, coming from an open bathroom window in the basement, drew him up short.

"Ow!"

Aleja.

Waving at the night security guard, he jogged through the door to the work site and toward the bathroom.

"Hello?" he called. His boots echoed on the cement floor, which was now stripped of the tacky carpet that had probably been installed when his mom was a kid. "Aleja?"

She didn't reply.

Heart punching his ribs, he flew into the bathroom. "Is everything—"

Aleja knelt on the ground of the otherwise empty room, unhurt, but at war with the orange ceramic flooring.

She's fine. Everything is fine.

His pulse thrummed, not getting the memo.

"Hey," he said, leaning against the door frame as if he hadn't raced in like he'd expected to find her bleeding out on the tile. "We meet again."

"Twice in one day." The words were muffled behind her dust mask.

Three times, if he counted her watching him remove icicles.

He decided he would.

Strong arms flexed as she pried her next target with a long, thin tool. The bathroom was big enough for two stalls and two sinks, though all the barriers and fixtures had been removed. She was half done stripping out the tiles. Curls escaped her braid, the sweaty tendrils framing her face.

He had enough—just enough—self-control to hold back from whimpering in appreciation. "I heard you swear, and—"

"And you can't not run to someone's rescue."

"Well… Yeah."

Watching her lift ugly ceramic squares was mesmerizing. The skill of it, for one. Also, because he had a pesky habit of memorizing her form. With those work overalls, it was hard to tell she was having a baby. But he'd paid too much attention to her over the years to miss the early, subtle changes in her body. A little softer, fuller. A whole lot of stunning.

"Mother…of…*pearl*…" A tile went flying, pinging off the wall. She crouched on her heels and looked up at him. "If you're going to hover, do it with a tool in your hand. These things aren't lifting by themselves. Some genius glued them on without subflooring."

"I can do grunt work."

Her gaze drifted from his face to somewhere around his biceps or chest. "Assumed you could. Toolbox is outside the door. Masks and eye protection, too."

He got the requisite tool and safety equipment and joined her, attacking the task from the opposite side of the room.

Popping the edge of the tool under a corner, he pried. It didn't budge.

Another jerk of his wrist. Nothing.

"What the hell?" he said.

"I know. They're the creation of Lucifer. Both in color and adhesion. Don't worry about leaving divots and scrapes—there's no other way. I'll refinish the concrete tomorrow."

With a crack, the tile finally gave way. *Phew.* He didn't care she was five times faster than him—it was her job, after all—but he wanted to come across as at least somewhat competent.

The wedge of lurid orange between them narrowed until they were a yard apart from each other.

She put her tool down, glaring at the remaining orange strip through her protective glasses. "I need a drink of water. Excuse me for a second."

He dug into the task, finishing it off before he realized he hadn't seen Aleja in twenty minutes. Huh. He spent another five minutes cleaning up what he could—they were going to need wheels of some sort to get the garbage can overflowing with cracked tiles out to the massive waste bin—and went to find her to let her know he was done.

Turning the corner into what would be the downstairs great room, he found it empty but for Aleja, sprawling in a plastic chair, head tilted back against one of the remaining studs. Her mouth hung open a bit, her arms loose at her sides.

Damn, he wasn't the only tired one.

"Aleja," he said in a low voice. "Alejandra."

Nothing.

Wait. Was she sleeping? Or had she passed out? It could be carbon monoxide... No. The alarm wasn't going off.

Plus, he remembered pranking her sleepovers with his sister. Nora would be awake all night like she always was, and Aleja would be dead to the world.

Kneeling at her side, he shook one of her shoulders. "Aleja." He took one of her wrists. Her pulse thrummed a strong beat under his fingers. Relief washed through him. "Wake up."

She jolted, grasping his biceps to avoid falling off the chair. The touch warmed his skin, even through his clothes.

"Huh? What?" Her dark brown gaze was wild, confused.

"You fell asleep," he whispered. "Time to go home."

"But we're not done."

"Yeah, we are. I finished up."

Her hand tightened on his arm. "Oh, my goodness, I owe you. You're a gem."

His heart tripped over itself. Would she still think that if she knew he'd had a crush on her since he was eleven, give or take?

"Nah. Get yourself home safe so that C shift doesn't need to come rescue you from a ditch, and we're square." He frowned. "You're not too tired to drive? I could run you into town, if you need."

Her thumb stroked idle circles above his elbow.

It would be way too easy to get used to her touch.

Eyes widening, she released her grip and stood. "I'll stay awake, Gray."

"I sure hope so. I'll see you tomorrow."

And the day after. And the day after that. If he made it to freaking *May* without clueing in Aleja to how much he wished he had a chance with her, it would be a miracle.

The next morning, Alejandra sat next to her grandmother in the waiting room of the fertility and birthing center, waiting for her ultrasound appointment.

Her phone buzzed in concert with her thrumming pulse.

Nora: Oh, sure, you'll take your abuela but not me ;)

You're working, she typed back. If Nora started taking time off to go to Bozeman with Aleja, people would ask questions.

Next time, okay? I want to be there for you.

Okay. The mid-pregnancy one has your name on it.

Her stomach jolted with its usual morning rebellion, and she held a fist to her mouth.

Abuela reached into her purse and handed her a tin of ginger droplets. "Keep them."

"Thanks."

"You should ask for a prescription. No need to suffer. You're already taking on more than many."

She glanced around the waiting room, at the glowing people with various sizes of pregnancy bellies and their happy partners.

She was the odd one out.

Her phone vibrated again.

Nora: Send me a pic of my nibling as soon as you can. Can't wait.

Chuckling at Nora's use of gender-neutral slang for niece or nephew, she typed, Just a few more minutes.

Seeing the picture—seeing her *baby*—would make it more real, even though the pregnancy symptoms and her slightly rounded belly were plenty of evidence.

A technician came into the waiting room. "Alejandra Brooks Flores?"

Aleja and Adelita rose and joined the woman.

"I'm Joanne," she said curtly, not the welcome she was used to getting from the people who worked here. "Come with me."

Soon after, Aleja was lying on a bed with a surgical drape over her knees, trying to pretend she was out for a Sunday stroll instead of being probed internally.

Abuela sat in a chair next to the exam table, legs crossed, expression contemplative. Every minute or so, she rubbed Aleja's arm.

Why was the tech looking so stern? The screen wasn't turned to Aleja yet. She really wanted to see what Joanne was seeing.

She exchanged a glance with Abuela.

Those knowing brown eyes were a balm, as was the quiet "It will be okay, Alejita."

She inhaled deeply. "Everything looking all right, Joanne?"

It was impossible to get a read off Joanne's flat lips. "Let me finish the last few frames and I'll get your doctor to talk to you."

"Is something wrong?" A wave of nausea hit, nothing to do with morning sickness. There were no guarantees with IUI. She'd chosen the method because it came with a much smaller price tag than IVF, accepting it didn't have the same success rate. It would have taken her years longer to save for the more complicated procedure, and she'd been eager to be a mom. She'd taken medication to increase her fertility hormones. But even at that, the first round didn't take. Had something gone wrong again?

Abuela took her hand and squeezed. Thank God she had insisted on coming today. Aleja would be better able to receive bad news with a steady, loving presence at her side.

Tears burned her eyes. "I was hoping this second round would work," she told Joanne. "I've been so sick, and gaining weight already..."

Joanne smiled woodenly and removed the ultrasound device. "You're pregnant. But there are a couple things the doctor's going to need to talk to you about."

Aleja tried to breathe, to find calm, but it didn't work. A drumline beat in her ears.

The tech typed for a minute then handed Aleja a box of tissues. "You can put your pants back on. Dr. Lopez will be right in."

A lump the size and hardness of a sledgehammer head crowded her throat. It threatened to dissolve, but she swallowed it down instead.

"I can do this," she croaked, hands shaking as she pulled her jeans on and sat back on the bed.

Abuela murmured in agreement.

"It'll take me another year to foot the bill for another round of IUI, or a couple of years if I want to try IVF instead, but I'm only thirty-six, and—"

There was a knock at the door, and Dr. Lopez entered, her white lab coat over a patterned wrap dress and tights. Aleja loved the care she'd gotten from her doctor so far. She'd expected to be questioned about taking on single parenthood while having a demanding job, but Dr. Lopez was a single parent herself and had been excited to facilitate Aleja's choices. It was comforting to be under the care of a woman who had to balance family and work, and still supported Aleja's decision to have a child.

Nor had she hidden how heartbreaking it would be if things went wrong...

Today, the doctor's brown eyes were smiling behind her glasses, and her merlot-red lips were curved up at the corners. "Buenos días, Aleja, Doña Adelita. So good to see you again."

Was she legitimately happy? Or was she pretending to avoid alarming Aleja?

"Dr. Lopez—"

"No need for that face, Alejandra. Today's a good day."

A good day.

"See?" Abuela said. "Todo está bien."

The urge to cry was stronger now than when she'd thought something was wrong. "But the tech looked so grim..."

"She's new. Worried about giving something

away, I think. I'll talk to her," the doctor explained. "I'm sorry she gave you the wrong impression. I'm glad you brought company. I have something amazing to show you."

"Amazing," Adelita echoed with another hand squeeze.

Dr. Lopez turned the screen to face the bed. "See? A good day. Heartbeats." She pointed at one little flicker, then another.

Adelita gasped.

"Wait." Aleja's thoughts skipped and stuttered worse than her aging truck's engine when it struggled to turn over. "*Two* heartbeats?"

"Yes, two."

"Mellizos," Adelita exclaimed.

"Exactly." Dr. Lopez's smile widened.

Aleja couldn't manage a single word. *Twins?*

Brown eyes, as familiar as Aleja's own, locked on her. "Say something, mi corazón. Are you okay?"

Corazón. Heart. "N-not one heart. *Two.*"

The doctor nodded. "Not what you expected, I know. But as we talked about prior to the procedure, there is a higher chance with the fertility meds."

Twins.

The word lodged in her brain, somewhere between *I am so, so alone* and *Madre de Dios, this is a blessing.*

Two babies, at the same time.

By herself.

Her skin tightened, hot and itchy.

Dr. Lopez's hand was cool on her wrist. "We'll go

over what this'll mean for your pregnancy. Delivering earlier, needing more support at work, adjusting your on-the-job duties—"

The list crashed over Aleja like a tsunami. Long-term, figuring out how to single-parent twins would be a hell of a thing. Short-term, her seven-month window for her construction project just shrank significantly.

She groaned.

"One day at a time," Abuela said.

"Time… Exactly what I'm worried about." She had resources and family support, but this contract was supposed to differentiate her from the rest of the builders in the area, including her dad. What would happen if she couldn't finish it?

The doctor smiled encouragingly. "I'll prescribe you something for your nausea. And I'll get you a printout of the scan. Got to have one for the baby album, right?"

"Right." Aleja's head buzzed. The rest of her body tingled. Her grandmother's firm grip was the one thing keeping her anchored to reality.

She was still in a daze when she pulled into the driveway of the cute little bungalow she and her dad had built for Adelita about a decade ago. It was down the gravel drive from the main ranch house where her parents lived, and across a wide field from her brother Rafa's place.

A smooth hand, scented as always with aloe vera moisturizer, cupped her cheek. "Are you going to go tell your parents?"

She shook her head. "I...need to process."

Two babies.

Delivering in July.

Off work other than basic walk-throughs by early June.

"Abuela," she whispered. *"Twins."*

"You have an unlimited capacity to love, Alejandra. I promise."

She had no choice but to believe her.

Her knuckles ached on the steering wheel as she turned onto the road that edged the lake all the way to the lodge. *Come on, Aleja. You make plans for a living. This is just one more.*

A warning light blinked at the edge of her vision: *This is not your average plan.*

Oh, wait, no. An actual light was illuminated on her dash. The same one that had been flickering on and off for a couple of weeks now, but it'd been Christmas holidays and then prep for starting the lodge renos, so it had seemed like it could wait.

And now there was a light blinking, and she had a few thousand dollars' worth of construction equipment on the seat behind her and a crew waiting for her and *two* tiny sprouts in her belly—

The engine went silent.

Aleja's pulse jolted. She swore and tapped the brakes. *Oof.* Stiff and hard to press. Okay, she'd glide, then, and hope to hell to come to a stop before the windy mountain road took a forty-five degree turn ahead. There wasn't much of a shoulder, so she pulled her truck over as much as she could, arms tensing as she fought the lack of power steering.

The tires crunched to a stop right before she would have had to steer around the bend in the road. *Phew.*

Hand shaking, she put the truck in Park.

Resting her forehead on the steering wheel, she groaned. There was no point in her trying to figure out the problem. She could make pretty much anything out of wood, but engines were a mystery. Got nothing but grief from her more mechanically minded brother and sisters.

Nor could she afford to wait for a tow. She'd missed enough work this morning. She was about a mile away from the lodge, easily walkable, but leaving the new saw in the cab would be asking for a break-in.

All right, who to call for a ride? Abuela would already be in town at her book club. Her dad was supervising a different building site, her younger sister was at the physical therapy clinic and her mom and brother were both busy with the ranch.

Nora had been around to text this morning, though… She pulled up their thread and asked, Are you nearby?

The reply came a minute later. Out checking fences. But I'll be ready with the celebratory sparkling apple juice at 6.

Nix asking for a rescue, then. Aleja wasn't going to pull Nora away from something important.

She'd have to call someone from her crew.

Her nose stung and her throat pinched. There

was no guarantee she wouldn't dissolve on the spot when she opened her mouth to ask for a favor. *Not the image she liked to project with her employees.*

Five minutes. Calm down. Then call.

She got out of her truck, boots squeaking in the packed inch of accumulation on the road. She took a pine-scented lungful of air and willed the lump in her throat to dissipate. The road followed the curve of the lake, providing a stunning view across the black, icy surface to the more inhabited side. She leaned against the driver's door and inhaled deeply a few more times.

It's okay to be a little late.

With Gray's help last night, she'd stayed on schedule. She'd also managed to fall asleep in a chair...

Her cheeks were still burning from that humiliation. Thank goodness it had been Gray who'd found her, not Emma.

Nora always talked about him like he was spoiled, an impression Aleja had gotten back when he was a teenager, and she was working her way up in her dad's business. She hadn't spent much time with him since he went off to college, though, or in the couple of years he'd been firefighting in town. Between him working for Emma on his days off and pitching in with the world's worst bathroom tile last night, all signs pointed to him having grown up a hell of a lot.

Sign number one: the way his shoulders stretch his T-shirt.

Sign number two: the I-know-how-to-pleasure-a-woman tilt to his mouth.

Her growl of frustration echoed off the surrounding trees. She had zero time to appreciate her best friend's little brother, even in secret.

She could thank her wandering thoughts for one thing, at least—her urge to cry was gone. She took one last, long breath, soaking in the calm of the forest. Snow, sliding off branches with muted *whump*s. The call of a hawk. A mewling cry from a shallow embankment on the other side of the road.

The hair rose on the back of her neck. Predators sometimes mimicked wounded animals to lure in prey.

Another whimper.

No, that was distress, not mimicry. Tiny, but real.

She scanned the area, trying to pinpoint where it was coming from. A dark green lump caught her eye, perched on the edge of a slope bordered with safety fencing.

The lump moved. *What the...?*

Aleja hurried across the road, stopping short of a reusable grocery bag, marked with the logo of Sutter Creek's local supermarket. The fabric shifted again, in tandem with a weak snuffle. Her stomach grew heavy with horror.

If there was a wounded animal in there, it could lash out at her if she tried to help. But she couldn't just leave it.

She stretched out a careful hand and lifted the edge of the bag. A ball of mostly brown fur was curled far inside. Impossible to tell what the animal was. She grabbed her cell from her pocket, flicked on the flashlight app and beamed it into the bag.

Two shiny eyes stared at her from a tiny canine face. A puppy, couldn't be more than a couple of months old. Maybe fewer.

Fury twisted inside her. "Oh, no. Pobrecita. What are you doing here?"

Chapter Four

Aleja jammed her phone back in her pocket and reached into the bag, murmuring nonsense as she gingerly removed the mewling creature. Barely two handfuls, it was shivering hard enough Aleja had to tighten her grip. A thin white star marked the brown face between its eyes. It had short fur, a few palm-size cocoa-brown patches on its body and four mottled legs and paws—

Wait.

Three paws. One of its front legs was misshapen, missing anything resembling a foot. Didn't look like a healing injury. Must have been born that way. "Did some lowlife desert you, sweetheart?"

The dog's cries pealed louder.

"Shh, shh, I got you."

Aleja took off her scarf and swaddled it around the miserable little love, like she used to do with her nephew when he was colicky. She unzipped the top of her jacket and nestled the dog inside.

By the way the dog snuggled close, she figured it would have crawled inside her to get warm if it could. She fastened her jacket as best as she could and jogged to her truck to use up whatever heat remained from before the engine died.

She had her phone in her hand and was ready to start dialing her crew, one by one until someone answered, when she caught the roar of an engine approaching from behind her.

Her pulse kicked up. Was it the deserter, returning to make sure the job was done?

She glimpsed blue paint through the trees. Her nerves released their grip on her throat. With that blue, chances were it was a truck from the Halloran ranch. She got out of her own vehicle and stood by the tailgate, keeping the dog against her collarbones.

The older-model Ford F-350, emblazoned with the RG Ranch logo, slowed as it neared Aleja. Heaped, tied-down furniture and boxes filled half the truck bed. Gray was behind the wheel, brawny and golden and looking far too much like the able rescuer she needed.

He parked behind her and jumped out, smiling with a flash of teeth that no doubt laid waste to the twentysomething population of Sutter Creek on the regular. "Truck troubles? Need a jump or something? Or a second set of eyes?"

She shook her head. "I don't think it's something we can deal with on the side of the road. The engine cut out on me."

"A ride, then." Another cheeky smile, one suggesting he didn't mind if she took his comment the exact wrong way.

Her face got hot. She had no business thinking about Graydon Halloran taking her on that kind of ride, but when he looked at her with feigned innocence—

She stiffened. First, the dog. Then, work. Then sparkling apple juice with Nora, or freaking out about her ultrasound, maybe. But whatever it was, it wouldn't involve Gray.

"A ride would be great. I'd have walked, but I couldn't carry a concrete saw all that way."

Reality struck. If she hadn't gotten out of her truck, she'd have never noticed the deserted animal. The puppy wouldn't have made it...

Tears threatened at the corners of her eyes. "Wait, though. I need to get to the vet, not to the lodge."

"The vet?"

"Yes, can you drive me to Maggie Reid's clinic? I know you're in the middle of moving, but...I found a puppy. Someone left it. I was coming back from Bozeman because I had a doctor's appointment and I found out...I'm having—" Nope, she couldn't say it yet. "I mean, my truck died while I was driving. I got out for a bit of air, and I heard a sound and—"

"Hey." One soothing word, combined with two gloved hands stroking her upper arms through her coat. Steady, supportive. "Where's the puppy?"

She unzipped her coat a little to show him her discovery. "It's—" Tears ran down her cheeks, turning from hot to cold. "It's been a morning."

"Oh, man. Would you look at that. So small." Thermal fleece–covered fingers wiped at the wet tracks. "Is this why you're upset? Or did something happen at your doctor's appointment?"

Something resembling a sob escaped. Damn it. She didn't have time to get weepy. And if she started talking about her ultrasound, she might never be able to stop crying. "I just want to get her to the v-vet. Can you take me?" She shifted her collar and the scarf, so those two dark eyes could steal his heart, too.

He sucked in air. "Is it a pointer of some kind? Looks like Lachlan Reid's dog."

"You're right." Lachlan's spotted search and rescue dog was famous around Sutter Creek for having the best nose in the woods. "Maybe he'll be at the vet clinic, too—both he and Maggie could take a look at the puppy."

"I can't believe someone *left it*," he said.

"I know."

He grimaced, muttering something his mother would have banished him from the dinner table for saying. Aleja had shared decades of meals with the Hallorans, and Georgie had a clear delineation between what was said in the barn and what was permitted at her table.

"Let's get going, then," he said. "Do you want to put your saw in the back? I could do that for you or hold the dog."

"You take the dog. I know what can't be left behind."

Widening his fingers, he indicated for her to hand him the shivering animal. She passed over her bundle of scarf and puppy.

Gray unzipped his winter jacket and cuddled the creature against his flannel shirt.

Her heart melted.

Back off, hormones. She slotted her boxes where there was room in the back, locked up as best she could and joined him in the cab.

The inside of the truck was loaded to the gills, including a box on the floorboards of the passenger seat. She caught whiffs of cumin, garlic and cinnamon, like a spice rack had crashed to a kitchen floor. He must have packed part of his pantry into one of the boxes in the crew cab. She crossed her legs as gracefully as she could manage.

"Sorry," Gray said, nuzzling the puppy. "Bit of a squeeze. I didn't want to risk my dry goods getting damp."

Guilt crept into her belly, twining around her perpetual nausea like a weed around a thornbush. "I shouldn't have asked for a favor."

"Happy to help. And look at this face." He frowned. "She's shivering so hard."

"Missing a paw, too," she said.

He peered at the dog's foreleg. "From birth, I'd say."

"I agree."

"We should hurry." He shifted the dog into her lap. **The puppy squirmed and squeaked.**

"Shh, baby," she murmured.

Gray's lightly tanned cheeks turned ruddy. "Uh, what?"

"The dog," she clarified, taking off her gloves. She lifted the dog from her scarf. It looked at Aleja with so much fear, the corners of her eyes prickled again.

"It's young. Probably barely weaned." Gray reached over, stroking one of its ears with a hand big enough to span the animal's length. "Let's get you some help, Baby Yoda."

He put the truck in gear and drove to the nearest crossroads to turn around.

"Baby Yoda!" Aleja nested her scarf in her lap and cradled the little creature, rubbing its velvet belly with a gentle fingertip. "She looks nothing like Grogu."

"Sounds like him, though." He petted the dog between the ears. His hand brushed Aleja's, the fleshy part of his palm streaking heat across her thumb.

Her breath caught. Since when did she react to Gray Halloran's skin on hers?

To distract herself, she texted her head carpenter to explain she'd be away from the site for longer than expected.

Way longer, based on Gray's current speed of ten under the limit.

"Going slow because of the load in the truck bed?" she asked.

"Yeah. And I'm transporting precious cargo."

Her skin tingled as the blood drained out of her

face. This morning was too much. The truck, the puppy, *twins*… She'd expected to return to the site and share her pregnancy with Emma, but with double the babies to share, it didn't feel so simple anymore.

"Precious cargo," she echoed.

"The dog, Aleja." He reached across and massaged one of the animal's tiny ears between a thumb and finger. Work-roughened hands. From firefighting now, but ranch work, too. He'd been pitching hay around the same time he started riding a tricycle.

The care of his touch melted her.

Gray took the next corner at a crawl.

Aleja's impatience surged. Maggie Reid's vet clinic was on the other side of town, and if the dog's snuffles turned to respiratory distress—

"She's feeling a little warmer. You're looking steadier yourself," he said. "You were pretty shaky when I picked you up."

"Adrenaline crash. When I heard the whimpers, I thought it might be a bobcat. And I'd better call for a tow. Today was always going to be busy, given my errands in Bozeman, but throw a busted truck and a puppy into the mix…"

"You'll manage. I've always believed you can handle anything," he said quietly.

He did? She fumbled with her cell. "Oh. Well, thank you."

After she placed the call and arranged for a tow, they chatted about their families as they drove through Sutter Creek. By the time Gray pulled the truck into the parking lot of the veterinary clinic, the dog had burrowed back against Aleja's chest.

She went to open the door, but Gray gripped her arm. "Wait. I'll come give you a hand down so you can keep her inside your coat."

"Such chivalry."

"Job of a firefighter. Opening doors for senior citizens and pregnant people."

"I'm not *that* pregnant yet. And I'm older than you, but not exactly retirement age."

"I know, I didn't mean—" He gritted his teeth. "Let me help you. We don't want the dog to get colder, and I don't want you to slip."

And she didn't want to come across as ungrateful after he'd gone out of his way to drive her here.

"Hey," she said when he got to her door and held out a hand to take her elbow. "I appreciate the favor."

His cheeks were pink. Might have been from the wind, but his satisfied smile suggested not. "Glad I was the first to drive by."

She had to admit she was, too. There was something irresistible about the crisp scent coming off his jacket as she slid from the truck.

She was well used to walking up the cement walk to the single-story house, converted long ago into the popular veterinary clinic. She'd spent months of her time on the property last year, both renovating the old barn out back into Lachlan's search and rescue dog school, and then rebuilding it after fire tore through it.

Gray held the door open for her and she entered

the cheery, tidy waiting area. Relief swamped her when she spotted a familiar tawny head behind the front desk. He had on a Gallatin Paws Foundation baseball cap and technical jacket.

"Lachlan! Am I glad to see you."

"Hey, my favorite contractor. Finally caving and adopting a pet?"

An antiseptic smell walloped her, cutting off her greeting. She fought off the temptation to bury her nose in Gray's jacket, in search of his soothing citrus scent.

Clearly, the prescription Dr. Lopez had given her took time to kick in. Nausea washed over her, making her light-headed.

Yikes. Legs weak, she swayed backward, landing against Gray's solid chest.

Not good not good not good. Step away from the burly steadiness.

Though Lachlan wondering why she was using Gray like a load-bearing wall was preferable to losing her balance.

"I'm sorry, I'm a bit dizzy, I—"

"It's okay." The low murmur kissed her skin, setting off an entirely different wave of tingles. "I've got you."

He did.

And she couldn't deny the truth—she liked it.

Gray almost had to shake himself to make sure he wasn't dreaming. Aleja Brooks Flores was using him as a physical pillar.

She wobbled, and he reflexively cupped her arms. Silky curls tickled his chin. This was moment-of-a-lifetime stuff, right here. If only her miserable nausea hadn't brought it on.

Right. It was time to fix the problem, not fantasize over an unavailable woman.

"What do you need?" he said.

"Sorry. It's, uh, the smell. Reminds me of blood. I'm not a fan." She straightened and turned to face him, expression silently begging him to support what he assumed was a lie.

"Blood phobia? Since when?" Lachlan asked. "You were fine last year when your plumbing subcontractor had that accident while working on the pipes in the barn."

"I can handle it in the moment." Her throat bobbed. "Oh, crap. Take the dog, Gray."

By the time he processed that there was a tiny animal in his hands, she was already darting past the reception desk and down the hallway.

Gray stared at the featherlight puppy, so small she barely filled his palms. She let out a thready whine. He brought the animal close, up around his chest like Aleja had been holding her. "Shh."

"If Aleja's needing a doctor, she might want the medical clinic," Lachlan suggested. "Though that little precious is up our alley. Who's the lucky dog parent?"

"We don't know. Aleja found it on the shoulder on the road to Emerson Lodge."

"On the *road*?" Lach bolted to his feet, his rangy

frame all efficient motion as he came out from behind the tall desk. His own dog followed, marked with brown and white spots and alert curiosity, nosing around Gray.

"Hands are full, here, doggo, if you're looking for a head scratch," Gray said to the animal.

"Fudge, off," the other man commanded gently before cursing. "Maggie stepped out with our receptionist to get lunch, begged me to answer the phone for her for a half hour."

"Can you take a look at her?"

"A cursory one, yeah." Lach had been a vet tech at the clinic before he'd opened his search and rescue dog training business. He pulled a phone from the pocket of his jeans and sent what looked like a quick text. "I let Maggie know to get back here pronto. But I'll do what I can."

"She looks like Fudge." Gray unwrapped the creature from Aleja's scarf and held it steady as the other man let out another low curse.

"Almost identical, but for the furrier face. She might be a wirehaired pointer. What the hell would lead a person to abandon—"

"She's missing a paw."

Lach examined the dog's face and front legs. "Not from abuse. May I?" He held out his hands to take the animal.

"Of course."

"I'll take her to an exam room," the other man said. "Do you want to see if Aleja's okay? She didn't look so hot."

Knowing he wasn't the only person concerned about her felt like a free pass to be nosier than she probably wanted. He nodded. "Is the washroom in the back?"

"Yup. I'll be in room three."

Gray strode down the blue-painted hall, stopping when he got to the closed washroom door at the back of the clinic. The door was thin enough it didn't block the sound of her throwing up.

"Alejandra?" he called. "I don't mean to lurk out here being weird, but are you okay?"

A grumbling moan filtered through the door.

He winced. "I'll go. Lach's checking out the dog. I'll make sure he doesn't need anything."

"Wait," she called.

The sink ran, and the door opened. She held up a hand. "Don't say anything. I'm embarrassed enough as it is."

"Nausea's normal, isn't it?"

"Yes, but it's screwing me over. I wanted to keep this under wraps for a while, though goodness knows it's impossible to keep anything a secret around here."

He hoped she didn't plan to hide things much longer. With her coat unzipped, the physical evidence was there, too. Her T-shirt didn't disguise the extra cup size or two, or her little bump.

Reaching for her, he stroked her shoulders with his thumbs. She was an intoxicating mix of athleticism and softness. Lush, but strong as hell from wielding power tools all day. Heat tightened low in his belly. Par for the course anytime he envisioned Aleja carrying a drill or circular saw. "Your secret's still safe. Lachlan bought your blood excuse, and I won't say a word."

Her breath quickened as she stared at him. "Never thought you were Mr. Trustworthy, but I think I was wrong."

Go figure, the first moment he felt like she was fully seeing him, it was after finding out she was irrevocably tied to some other lucky human.

"Color's back in your face." Better not to address her epiphany.

"Yeah, I'm good now."

He released her shoulders. His heart panged. She was involved with someone else, having a baby with them. He wouldn't get another chance to touch her for a long while. "We should go check on the furry peanut."

A hand flew to her mouth. "Of course!"

He motioned in the direction of the exam rooms.

They entered the room where Lachlan had taken the puppy. Gray stepped to the side so she could enter first.

"How are things looking?" she asked, joining Lachlan at the waist-high table. He had the puppy resting under a blanket on what appeared to be a heating pad. The tiny eyes were closed, face disgruntled. An old soul. Lachlan was checking her with a stethoscope.

Gray stood a couple of yards back. No need to overwhelm the creature.

"You did good to warm her through body heat," Lach said. "Her temperature is almost where it should be, and her heart rate is improving."

Aleja smiled, gentle and relieved. She bent low and leaned her elbows on the table, petting the dog's head and front paw. Instead of a whimper, the animal let out a contented snuffle. "She'll be okay?"

"I'm going to let Maggie make that call. She'll need to run tests, check for any aftermath from substandard care. But she might be well enough to go home tonight." Lachlan palmed the top of his head. "Provided you're claiming her, Aleja."

"I— A dog—"

"A tripod, at that," Lach said seriously. "Bit more care involved. Sometimes we can arrange fostering or adoptions, but this one'll be trickier."

Aleja's face fell. Her hand stilled on the dog's head. "I want to, but I don't know. My hours are heinous, and I'm going to— I mean, I have a few other things—"

Other things like expecting a baby. No wonder she was hesitant.

"I'll take her," Gray blurted.

Aleja's gaze jerked to his. "The dog?"

He nodded. "If you're okay with it."

"Graydon…" The wonder on her face filled him enough he thought he'd float home.

"You sure, man?" Lachlan studied him. "Speaking of people with heinous hours. You can't leave her home alone for a twenty-four-hour shift."

He sent the other man a you-don't-say look. He'd

worked with the dog handler many times when the search and rescue team paired up with the fire department. Gray knew the concern came from a real expertise with canines, but it stung to be underestimated by someone he considered a colleague of sorts. "Yeah, I know what I'm offering. But I have some favors I can call in with a work buddy. His wife runs a doggy daycare for some of the other people who work at the firehouse. And my mom can pitch in if I'm in a bind."

"What about the lodge?" Aleja said.

Gray winced. "Right. I should check with Emma."

He pulled out his phone. People are still bringing hunting dogs to the lodge, right?

A few seconds later, Emma responded. For now, yes. And I'd expect we'll get a few that are a part of wedding ceremonies. Why?

I'm adopting one. A mind trip, but it felt like the best thing to do.

WHAT? YOU?

Thx for the vote of confidence, he replied, then put his phone away. "The lodge allows dogs."

Nodding, Lachlan took its temperature again. "All right, then. Maggie will call you when she's completed her exam."

Holy hell, he'd adopted a pet. "I— Yeah. I should finish moving in if I'm going to provide her with any semblance of a home."

"Give me a half hour to make sure my crew is on

task, and I'll come help you unload," Aleja offered, still stroking the dog's silky ears. "It's the least I can do after hijacking your day."

"You didn't." His voice turned gruff. He edged closer to the table, sidling up to Aleja. Mimicking her elbows-on-the-table posture, brushing shoulders with her in the process, he lowered his face to get close to the—*his*—puppy. He petted the top of her head with two fingers. The fur there was softer than on the rest of her little body. "I'll come back and get you, okay? Someone else might have left you, but I won't."

When he stood, he caught a glint of moisture in Aleja's eyes.

He cocked an eyebrow.

Her tawny cheeks turned pink. "She's cute, okay? And I was worried."

"So was I." Suppressing the need to lean in and kiss her forehead—the dog wasn't the sole source of cuteness in the room—he shook Lachlan's hand. "I'll be back as soon as you need me." He glanced at Aleja. "Are you sure you're feeling well enough to haul a bunch of boxes around?"

She bristled. "I haul beams on a daily basis—I can handle your flannel collection."

He laughed. Preferable to groaning. He wasn't sure he could manage having Aleja in his space without letting on he'd been dreaming about that very reality for years.

Chapter Five

Aleja was back in the passenger seat of Gray's truck, legs crossed again to accommodate the box at her feet. He was driving with one wrist on the top of the wheel and a hand on the shifter. She stared at the road, not wanting yet another example of how Nora's younger brother had somehow strolled into hot territory while she wasn't looking,

Aleja had been in *fifth grade* when he was born.

It had to be the way he'd held and talked to the dog. Spoke to her maternal hormones. What other explanation was there for it?

Uh, everything about him?

The shoulders, sculpted by hours hauling fire hoses. The smile, marred perfectly by a tilt. The rugged Carhartt-jacket-and-jeans style, so familiar to her from being on work sites, but somehow extra delicious on Graydon. Each time he moved, commanding but easy in the space his big frame demanded, he drew her in.

They passed the point on the road where she'd left her truck. It was gone—she'd gotten a text from the tow company before she'd left the vet clinic.

"Freddy already came with the tow?" Gray asked. "Quick service."

"We took over an hour. Long enough for you to adopt a puppy."

Guilt pinched her throat. Aleja had found the dog. Heck, she'd *wanted* to take her. But twins... Two infants wouldn't leave her with any time to pee or shower, let alone take care of a dog.

"Yeah. I did that." His mouth twisted into something resembling bewilderment. He ran a hand through his wavy hair, messing it to tousled-and-touchable.

"You're sure you can manage?"

Hurt flashed in his blue eyes. "Of course, I am."

"Sorry. I just didn't want you to feel obligated because I couldn't take her myself. I feel badly I can't step up."

"You don't need to explain it, Alejandra."

Had he always caressed the vowels of her name so thoroughly? He usually called her Aleja, but when he dragged out all the syllables, managing the Spanish lilt... What else could he manage with his tongue?

The world whooshed by—the lake on the left and

forest on the right—and with it, all her preconceived notions of her relationship with Graydon Halloran.

He looked a little flushed around the collar as he slowed in the turning lane to the lodge. The bulky log arch with Emerson Wilderness Lodge burned into the wood still framed the entrance to the private road.

"Got a plan to freshen the entranceway?" he asked as they drove under it.

"Of course. I have a plan for every inch of the property." Working with Emma on turning the lodge into a wedding facility was going to let her spread her artistic wings in a way she hadn't been able to do, given her dad's more utilitarian bent. She loved working with her dad. Joe Brooks had taught her everything she needed to start off in the business. He'd also pushed her to expand her skill set beyond his expertise. Every minute she'd spent honing her craft would be worth it to see the heritage lodge both preserved and revitalized. "Emma's signed off on my vision. I have a surprise for her for the main hall, though." She was counting on building a stunning floor with a load of mountain pine beetle lumber, if she could get it.

"You're full of secrets," he mused, winking at her.

Her palms dampened. "I—"

"Any fascinating woman is, Aleja."

"I'm worried your sister will find out about my... other surprise...and won't want me on the job anymore."

"Ah, yeah," he murmured.

"You think I'm right to worry?" She'd faced too many stereotypes in her industry to trust her pregnancy wouldn't influence Emma's decision. Especially with expecting multiples. She and Dr. Lopez had talked about best, worst and most likely scenarios, and none of them involved her working until week thirty-eight like she'd planned with what she thought was a singleton pregnancy. She could go from now until July as healthy as anything, or she could end up on bedrest like her mom and sister had when they were pregnant. And she wasn't even at the three-month mark, where the lessened risk for potential miscarriage meant she could breathe easier, either.

The lodge came into view, both soaring and homey. Its log exterior was a dream, and come spring, the landscaping crew she'd subcontracted would have a veritable forest to craft into something wildly cultivated.

By then, she'd be six months along but looking full-term. *Yikes.*

She worried a hangnail on her thumb and tried to release the tight muscles in her ribs. Her waistband was feeling too tight, too. At least now she knew why she was already showing.

"Emma's driven, but she's a romantic," he finally said. "She's also big on giving other women opportunities."

"I'm counting on that."

He bypassed the main parking lot and steered down the narrower lane leading to parking spots along the far side of the lodge. He pulled into the space closest to a door. Shifting his truck into park with a steady hand, he said, "It'll all work out."

She met his sincere, too-blue gaze. "I hope you don't think I'm misleading Emma. I just… I can do this. And I don't want to be underestimated."

Nodding, he turned off the engine. He brushed her cheek with a roughened hand, sending a shiver along her skin. "You don't know how much I understand what you mean."

That touch promised she could trust him.

It threatened she couldn't trust herself *with* him.

Forty minutes later, Aleja swerved through the door to Gray's suite, arms full of half of his easy chair. He was walking backward, not even close to breaking a sweat.

"You sure it's not too heavy?" he said.

So far, he'd restrained himself from questioning her ability to lift things. With the studio-apartment-sized room mostly furnished, the chair was the only piece of furniture requiring teamwork.

She glared at him. "Nothing the size of a gummy bear—" *two gummy bears* "—is going to stop me from carrying a chair."

His gaze dropped to her T-shirt covered bump, no longer hidden by a sweatshirt. "A gummy bear?"

They clomped over to the space he'd cleared next to a wide window.

"So I've read," she said.

"Sure it's not a whole bag of them?"

She almost dropped the chair on her toe. *"What?"*

He winced. "Sorry. You look fantastic. Really. But with your jacket and hoodie off, it's kind of obvious."

"Son of a—" She finished with a growl instead of a curse. That *fantastic* in no way made up for equating her itty-bitty bump to something larger.

"It'll be okay," he said. "Just…keep your hoodie on."

He guided them another yard back and they set the chair on the ugly carpet. Eventually, he'd have to move because the loft suites were part of the renovation. She'd have it transformed from '70s-fishing-hut to sumptuous, romantic retreat in no time.

She stood in the middle of the space. The room was chilly from the open window, cooling the sweat on her arms. "I was planning to talk to my crew soon. But after my ultrasound, I'm not sure."

"I understand feeling stressed about it. One of the women on my shift was pregnant last year. It was complicated for her, juggling a physical job she loved but also wanting to keep herself and her baby safe."

He approached, stopping close enough for her to smell lime rind and sunshine. He was in a T-shirt, too, and his shoulders strained the cotton. A straight-from-the-big-screen, golden superhero, except a thousand percent real and standing in front of her.

He lifted a hand close to her cheek but dropped it before making contact. A shadow flickered in his eyes. "I'm happy for you. And for the father."

"The fath— *Oh.*" She shot Gray a half smile. "I'm not with anyone. It's only me. And science. Science is pretty great."

His mouth slowly parted, until he gaped at her.

Defensiveness licked hot behind her ribs. "I didn't expect you to judge."

"I'm not!" He lifted his hands, palms forward. "I'm just surprised."

She didn't know what to say. People were going to be surprised she'd chosen single parenthood. She'd been having imaginary conversations for weeks, rehearsing her explanations for friends, nieces and nephews, extended family in California and Mexico.

His buzzing phone saved her.

He answered. "Oh, hey, Maggie—" He smiled, and Aleja breathed in relief. He said a few more *uh-huh*s and *great*s and then "sure, okay," before hanging up. "I have a small-but-healthy dog to retrieve in an hour."

"Good luck," she said. She knew she'd wanted someone to say the same to her this morning when she found out her news.

Maybe she needed to force the words past her nerves.

She finally let herself touch her stomach. "I'm having twins."

He stilled.

His gaze flicked over her shoulder, and he swore under his breath.

A similar oath came from the doorway, a higher, more feminine voice.

Emma Halloran. "*Twins?* Oh, my God. Gray. Are they *yours*?"

Chapter Six

Mine?

A flash of fantasy, of coming home from a shift and getting to wake both Aleja and a sleepy, cozy baby struck Gray hard enough to leave a mark.

Wait—*two of them*. She was having twins.

And in no way was she or her babies *his*. No matter how much his heart craved the image rooting deep in his chest. The possibility of loving her *and* her children was—

Impossible. It's impossible.

Right. And the longer he stood there with his mouth catching flies, not answering his sister, the higher the chance she or Aleja was going to correctly interpret the yearning he suspected was all over his face.

Aleja looked no more ready to respond—her mouth hung open as wide as his—but Emma was his sister, so this was his mess to clean up.

Forcing a blank look, he shook his head. "Of course, I'm not the father."

Aleja's dark gaze met his, marred by a flicker of something resembling hurt.

"Not that it wouldn't be a privilege," he clarified. *More than.* "I'm just… I'm sure you wouldn't want rumors starting—"

"Hey!" Emma crossed her arms over her winter coat. "I wouldn't gossip! Aleja's been Nora's bestie long enough to be family, and we don't treat family like that."

For crying out loud. "Also not what I meant." He modulated his voice, aiming for calm instead of the frustration and embarrassment gripping his throat. "We all know how quickly someone overhearing you telling Luke 'So I accused my brother of being the father of Aleja's babies—oops' turns into someone else relaying 'Emma thought Gray fathered Aleja's twins—oops' which turns into plain-old 'Gray fathered Aleja's twins—what an oops.' Which means a big mess for Aleja."

No child deserved to be labeled *Oops*, in utero or otherwise.

Aleja straightened. She settled her hand at her waist. The instinctive motion was another wallop to the chest for Gray. She was going to be a mom. A wonderful mom, protective and smart and loving.

"It'd be a mess for you, too," she said, eyes wide.

True. Talk about a scoop for the Sutter Creek gossip chain—between their age difference and Aleja and Nora's decades-long friendship, any connection between Gray and Aleja would be gold-level chitchat.

"Well, as long as I don't carelessly relay this misunderstanding, I don't see anyone making the connection between the two of you." Emma snorted. "Everyone's going to have a hard enough time believing you adopted a puppy, Gray, let alone being a dad to twins. Where is the lucky fur child, by the way?" Her sharp gaze scanned the room. "And won't you need a crate and food and—"

"I know how to care for a dog. I'm going to the pet store before I pick her up," he snapped. Shaking his head, he tried to regain his calm. "And we're getting off track. Aleja—I'm sorry my sister jumping to conclusions overshone your amazing news. Twins. Congratulations."

"Two babies. Exciting." Emma's words were genuine, but her eyes were wary. "I'm assuming you have a plan in place when it comes to you working?"

"I'll be making one." Aleja sent a nervous look at his sister. "I just found out this morning. Can you keep this between you and Luke for the time being?"

Emma nodded. "Definitely."

The mix of happiness and uncertainty made Gray want to gather Aleja in his arms and hold her until she felt like she was standing on solid ground again.

Given the demands of parenthood, that uncertainty might be for the rest of her life.

And he was totally open to the idea of getting to hold Aleja for that long.

Damn it, why couldn't he let go of that fantasy? She'd never even suggested interest. The last thing he intended to do was chase after an uninterested woman.

"If anything, my pregnancy is the ultimate guarantee the work will get done on time." Aleja's smile wavered and she backed toward the door. "That said, I should get back to my crew."

"And I need to get the puppy soon," he said, ripping tape off the box of books he planned to stack in the small bookshelf next to the bed.

"Enjoy your new baby." Aleja left, closing the door behind her.

Emma plunked down on the end of the bed and put her face in her hands. "Oh, my goodness. My contractor is pregnant with twins?"

"You told her it wasn't an issue," he reminded his sister.

"And it *isn't*—Mom ran a damn ranch while she was pregnant with all of us—but *twins?* She must be freaking out inside. You're going to be around the project—if you recognize she's having any problems, make sure to…" Emma made a face. "No, never mind. She knows how to take care of herself. I'd be infuriated to have some young guy claim to know something about my body more than I did."

"I'm not going to mansplain her pregnancy to her, Em. Promise." He raked a hand through his hair. "But if I can, I'll offer to help."

"Right. Good." Emma got an I-need-a-task look on her face. She shucked off her blazer, headed with a box toward the kitchenette and started unloading the few items he hadn't put in storage into the single cupboard over the one-basin sink.

Speaking of parts of the lodge in need of renovation: this room. Talk about outdated. A sheet of pea-green laminate counter topped the bar fridge next to the two-burner stove. Good thing he ate a lot of his meals at the firehouse, because making anything of substance would be impossible.

"I can't believe you adopted a dog."

He'd known this was coming. "Sometimes these things are meant to be, Em. Even if it means some inconveniences."

"Your work schedule is more than an inconvenience."

"I'm putting a call into my coworker's wife's doggy daycare as soon as I'm done unpacking."

A stack of plates landed in the cabinet with a clatter. "We need to make a plan for your shifts for me, too. I held off hiring someone else because I knew I'd have you part-time." She worried her lip. "Luke's grandpa liked having my cat with him over the holidays while I was consumed by the Christmas festival. Maybe he'd like a friend. Dog sit for you while you're doing maintenance work."

"That's a great idea," he said. Hank Emerson lived on the lodge property and was a big animal lover. "And thanks for the help with this, too."

She spent most of her day running around at superspeed. Implementing a vision like hers was no small thing—buying half ownership in the lodge and transforming it into a high-class wedding resort. Luke and Hank owned the other half, but the management was all Emma. She and Luke had been at loggerheads during the Christmas holidays, partly over the future of the lodge, partly because they'd both been too stubborn to admit they were falling in love.

Lifting a shoulder, she shelved his favorite mug. "You're allowed to move in more than a recliner, a shelf and a couple frying pans, you know."

"This bed's bigger than mine," he said with a shrug. "It's an upgrade. And Mom and Dad had plenty of room in the barn for the rest of my stuff." He didn't have much, anyway. Most of the furniture at his old place had belonged to his roommate, and he'd been living there since he finished his probationary period as a firefighter two years ago.

He was still the most junior member of the town's department but being the youngest and earning his place was as natural to him as breathing.

"I want it to feel like home for you, Gray," Emma said. "Until it's time to renovate this room, anyway. Then we'll have to move you to a cabin." She shook her head. "By that time, Aleja might be off work. I wonder if her dad will take over for her. But he's not as creative—"

"Trust her, Em. Once she processes the fact she's having twins, she'll adjust her schedule."

"Okay." Her voice was uncharacteristically small.

"And if I see any way to step in and help, I'll do it. You can trust me, too."

The doubt in his sister's eyes cut deep. But he'd find a way to prove her wrong.

The scrape of a shovel on asphalt greeted Aleja's ears as she parked her truck in the maintenance lot and climbed out into the nippy February air. A week had passed since the day she'd found the dog.

Since her doctor's appointment.

She'd spent the last seven days with the memory of those two heartbeats in her ears. The echo had kept rhythm alongside the pounding and hammering of construction. A week of dreaming of the future, and of trying to get her workers to speed up without being obvious about why she needed the productivity.

"There. We're done." A satisfied male voice came from the other side of the berm of snow at the end of the parking lot. "Want to get out now, Penny?"

Gray, talking to his dog.

Adorable. Aleja hoisted her bag over a shoulder, unable to suppress a smile.

"Hang on, sweetheart. Just wait," he said.

Aleja rounded the snowbank. Graydon wore winter gear. A furry lump wiggled on his chest, tangled in a pouch and straps.

"Shoot," he muttered, big gloved hands trying to untangle the dog's front leg from a strap. "Easy, Penny."

"Is that a baby carrier?" she asked.

Gray's gaze snapped up, and his cheeks went ruddy. "Uh, yeah. My doggy daycare person suggested I sew the leg holes shut so I can have her with me while I work. It was going a-okay until I tried to get Penny out."

A hulking guy cuddling a peanut of a puppy. Heart be still. "Post it on TikTok and you'd be famous."

"Famous for getting my dog stuck in a Baby-Björn? No thanks." But he laughed as he eased out another wiggling leg.

Aleja put down her tools and rushed forward, stopping right before the wall of his chest. "Here, I'll help."

Both Gray's embarrassed blue gaze and Penny's sparkling brown one fixed on Aleja, and she almost died from the sheer volume of cute.

Having used a baby carrier a bunch with her nieces and nephews, she undid a couple of clips and freed the dog's tangled limb. She lifted her from the cocoon and cuddled the furry body under her chin. "Oh, Gray. She smells like a puppy."

A corner of his mouth turned up as he untangled the straps of the carrier and put it back to rights. "Acts like one, too. Mainly in having ten-minute Animal-from-the-Muppets bursts of energy followed by an hour of solid sleeping. Hence the carrier."

"Adorable," Aleja said.

"Yeah?" Gray looked almost pleased at the possibility.

"The first time you take her to play on the lawn

of the town square, you're going to walk away with a month's worth of dates lined up. Guaranteed."

He frowned.

"Not on the market right now?"

"No… I mean, yeah, but—" He sighed. "I haven't been looking. Not for a while."

Huh. She'd have thought he'd have a line-up of interested women. But she completely understood not being in the place for a relationship.

"Me neither. For obvious reasons." She laid a row of kisses between Penny's ears. The dog wiggled, trying to nip at Aleja's chin. "No bites." She nudged the dog's nose, earning the puppy equivalent of a pout. "Oh, my goodness, none of that. You're going to have me regretting not adopting you myself."

"Any time you want to hang out with her, she's all yours."

He wasn't saying it in an *I'm exhausted and please get this creature off my hands* sort of way. More *eager to share the wealth.*

"You know, it'd be good for me to get some air and play with a puppy on my breaks."

Gray grinned. "You know where to find me."

She did. And the lightness in her chest at the thought of spending coffee breaks or lunch hours with him—with his dog, that was—made her happier than she'd anticipated.

Chapter Seven

Getting some puppy time during the day would have been entertaining, but it had been over a week since Gray had invited her to take a break during the day and Aleja had yet to find a spare minute. Today, she was driving down the road toward Sutter Creek, seething at her Bluetooth. "Run that by me again?"

Materials shortages weren't her father's fault, and he didn't deserve to be on the receiving end of Aleja's temper. But this was the first glitch the project had run into since they'd started framing and roughing in the basement, and she hadn't anticipated it.

"My drywall's late, too, Aleja," her dad said. "And it's only delayed a few days."

Breathe. That's manageable.

"Justifies taking part of the morning to argue with Cherry Franklin about permits," she said.

"I thought all that was taken care of." He sounded confused.

"No, this is for something new. Emma and Luke want to add a second story to one of the cabins. A starter house for them. My second crew will be freed up from the golf course job by next week, and I want to get them working. Smooth transitions."

The long pause felt like a scold.

"Dad?"

"That's a lot to take on, mija."

She bristled. "You've never questioned me before."

"You weren't pregnant with twins before."

Goddamn it, not him, too. And a change of tune since she'd revealed her news to her family the day after that monumental ultrasound. Her parents had been ecstatic over the possibility of another grandchild to love. "Being pregnant isn't going to hamper my ability to manage a project."

"It's okay to compromise. Especially with taking on parenting alone."

She gritted her teeth. She had the time to manage work and parenting *because* she wasn't in a relationship. All the decisions were hers. No getting caught unaware by a partner changing his mind about the most important things in life. One cancelled wedding was enough for her to be mighty cautious about traveling that road again.

"I have the project under control, Dad. Starting

with Cherry." Dealing with state permitting had been a cinch compared to the stubborn town hall clerk in charge of Sutter Creek's paperwork. She intended to get Cherry's full attention. No more *it's too close to the end of business hours* or excuses about the staff being shorthanded.

"Come over for dinner tonight. Rafa and I have carnitas on the smoker."

She shuddered at the thought of the meat dish she normally loved, but wasn't going to turn down the opportunity to see her family. "As long as Abuela's in charge of tortillas and beans, I'm all good. I'll see you then."

Saying goodbye to her dad, she pulled her truck into a spot behind one side of Sutter Creek's town square.

A minute later, she was standing in the Sweets and Treats line to get some cookies—fine, bribes—to act as permit lubricant.

The bakery was a hub of activity, mismatched tables jammed with locals and tourists who were skipping out on a day on the ski hill. The air was tinged with sugary frosting, chocolate and a hint of snow-damp clothing. A rainbow of painted hearts cascaded across the front window, along with "Happy Valentine's Day" in white script.

Joining the five-deep line, she held in a sigh. She couldn't remember the last time she'd celebrated the holiday. Casual dating didn't necessitate hearts and flowers. It had been seven years since she was last in a serious relationship. Initially, after calling off her wedding, the wounds of betrayal had kept her from connecting with someone new. But even after the jagged tears in her heart healed, she hadn't felt the urge to commit to a man. Life was easier when she wasn't vulnerable to someone else's changing whims.

When she didn't have to discover that what she thought was love was a lie.

Next year, though, she'd have two babies to dress in pink and red, to take to the Valentine's craft hour at the community center and make two footprint hearts with four tiny feet. She couldn't resist the smile pushing at the corners of her mouth.

Fourteen days to get used to the idea of twins, and it had only settled in on a surface level.

A menagerie of fluffy frosting and lacy baked goods overflowed from the glass case and cake stands decorating the counter.

Her stomach growled loudly enough that the person in front of her turned and gave her a startled look.

She scrunched her face in sheepish apology.

"Two things."

The low voice wasn't from the guy in front of her, but came from over her shoulder, as rich and buttery as the scent of pastry in the air. Gray's words curled around her like a hug, simple as they were.

She turned a little. "Two things?"

Two...pectorals. Oh, my. She was ill prepared for Graydon Halloran in a winter coat open over a tight navy polo shirt. And those navy uniform pants and black work boots... He was liable to cause an accident while walking down the street.

A smile crept over his face. "One—sounds like you skipped breakfast. And two—I'd like to rectify that."

"You want to buy me breakfast?"

His cheerful expression dimmed. Okay, maybe her tone had been fifty percent confusion, fifty percent shock, which was easy to mistake for a hundred percent snark. Or so Rafa liked to tell her. Having Gray look at her with his own confusion brought on the same sort of guilt as if she'd kicked his puppy.

She opened her mouth to say something in a gentler tone, but he jumped in first.

"You didn't take me up on my puppy-and-a-break offer. The fried egg sandwiches here are the best in town, in my opinion. I'd be happy to get you one."

"I'm here to get cookies for the municipal clerks, though, not something for me."

"Then you buy the cookies, and I'll get whatever you want."

She kept her voice low. "I can't do eggs. I'm still queasy. The medication my doctor gave me is working, but it's not infallible."

His expression grew more troubled. "You seemed like you haven't been feeling as ill." His eyes widened. "Not that I was looking for it or anything. I just—"

"Don't worry about it. I almost puked on you. Twice. It's not something you're going to forget."

Though she wouldn't have thought he'd notice how she'd been feeling from that point on.

"Anyway," she said, "If you're insisting—"

"I absolutely am."

"I'll have—" she scanned the case "—a cinnamon scone? That should sit okay."

He grinned. "You got it."

Wow. It was like standing in a full ray of sun. She warmed all the way to her core.

Oh, yikes. Too many complications, Aleja.

Even so, it was impossible not to smile back.

"What's with the cookies?" he asked after she put in her order.

She made a face. "Permitting's being difficult on the cabin Emma and Luke want overhauled. Sugar can't hurt."

"Sorry to hear that," he said, and then reeled off an order for eight different coffees and types of pastries that he must have had memorized for a while. "Tell me about the finished product."

They waited for their orders, and she explained the mix of rustic and modern she envisioned for his sister's new living space, mixing Luke's homey preferences and Emma's love of clean, simple lines.

"The whole property will have your touch on it," he said.

Excitement twinged in her belly. "That's the plan."

The server passed over a clear-topped box of cookies to Aleja. She wanted to get going, but her scone was mixed in with Gray's big order.

"Need help carrying that?" she offered. "I mean, I'm going that way anyway."

"No," he said. "I've got a system." The same server passed him two cardboard holders of four drinks, and a paper bag full of baked goods. "But I'll walk with you while you eat the scone."

Hands full with the drink trays, he nodded at the single paper bag on the high counter. "Yours."

"Thanks," she said, taking the treat and leading the way out.

No one was going to blink an eye at the two of them strolling from Sweets and Treats to the combined city hall/emergency services building off the Main Street square. The connection between their families—both her friendship with Nora, and Nora's ongoing feud with Rafael—was well established.

But *she* noticed. Gray's solid presence, their steps in tandem on the wood planks of the square's high sidewalks, the weight of his blue gaze resting on her for a little longer than usual.

And then there were her jeans, the waist held together with a MacGyver-style rubber band and safety pins. Yet another reminder that if their family connection wasn't enough of a reason to ignore how much she liked walking with him, her growing stomach sure was.

"Did you hear about the chimney fire we had to deal with yesterday?"

She shook her head and took a bite, letting the sweet cinnamon goodness melt over her tongue.

He shuddered. "Bats."

"During a fire? How?"

"We thought the problem was the owner feeding his desiccated Christmas tree into his woodstove. I mean, that was a problem—smoke damage, singed carpet—but once we doused the living room and realized there was a blocked chimney, we went on the roof to investigate. And boom—face full of bats."

"I don't know whether to laugh or cringe." Or be thankful that he hadn't been bitten or fallen off the roof.

"Both. I may have screamed like a little kid," he said as they turned onto a side street.

The municipal building came into view, a beautiful, multistory glass structure—that Brooks Contracting had unsuccessfully bid on with an architect friend of her dad's, dang it. She'd have loved to be a part of something so sweeping and eye-catching. The angles reminded her of an ice overhang, and the wood support beams of the trees. Perfect for a mountain town.

She swallowed the last bite of her scone. "My stomach thanks you."

"Didn't have time for breakfast?"

"Oh, I very much did. That was *second* breakfast," she joked. "My pregnancy appetite knows no bounds."

"I'll remember that tomorrow. Bring you something from the lodge kitchen for elevenses." He grinned.

She laughed at his reference to a hobbit's eating schedule. "You know, it's nice to have a few moments during the day where I can talk openly about it. Early pregnancy is weird—it's on my mind all the time, but it really doesn't impact anyone else at all. Not yet."

"When will you tell your crew?"

"Two more weeks, I think. To be safe," she said.

They walked through the automatic doors. Gray nodded at the receptionist.

He stopped short. "I'm through there." He nodded at a door on the opposite side of the atrium from the town services department. "I'll, uh, see you around."

Aleja could feel the receptionist's eyes tracking them. Or maybe she was just ogling Gray.

"Cross your fingers I make it to the top of the priority pile," she said.

"You got it."

She forced herself not to watch him walk away, rushing toward the municipal services wing instead. Unlike the receptionist, who was ogling his backside with unabashed zeal, Aleja couldn't risk publicly appreciating him.

The door closed behind her, and with it, temptation. A long counter bisected the high-ceilinged, airy space, dividing the waiting area from the scattering of desks and dividers where the staff worked. One person stood at the counter, ahead of her in the line. Sitting in the row of chairs by the window, she fidgeted with the sticker on the box of cookies. When she finally got called up, she went forward with an over-wide smile.

"Cherry." The older woman had added a brilliant magenta streak to her silver chignon since the last time Aleja had been in. It matched her bright lipstick. "Love the hair color. Great choice." Aleja passed the box over. "For your troubles, given how much work the lodge job is turning out to be."

Cherry pursed her lips. "I can't be bribed, honey. We deal with applications in the order they're submitted. You know this."

"Yes, but—"

"And with all I hurried on your permits on the lodge itself, I would have thought you'd have plenty to do without having to rush the other buildings." The clerk made a show of studying her cuticles.

Heat rose on the back of her neck. "Except—"

"You know, your dad never puts up a fuss like this."

Aleja almost covered her ears. Surely, steam had to be escaping.

A shadow appeared in the side of her vision. Great, she was seeing spots.

Two fit forearms leaned on the desk, an inch from her own arm.

Oh. Not spots.

A brawny, interfering firefighter. He took a sip from a bakery take-out cup and handed Cherry an identical version. "Extra vanilla syrup, like you prefer."

The older woman downright fluttered her eyelashes. "Thank you, sweet pea."

Gray leaned his weight on the counter and smiled sideways at Aleja. "I'm so glad my sister's contractor is in good hands with you, Ms. Franklin. We couldn't get the job done nearly so well without the town staff being so damn helpful."

Cherry flushed. "Well, you know how we like to keep Sutter Creek ticking. I was just telling Alejandra her application is almost at the top of the pile."

"You were?" Aleja had to keep her jaw from dropping at the blatant lie.

The fluttering lashes stilled. Brown eyes latched on to Aleja, simmering with warning. "Maybe by the end of the day if I'm able to get to things on time."

Oh, good grief.

Gray's mouth worked a little more magic, a flash of teeth and a stretch of lip that no doubt would taste as yummy as it looked—

Aleja dropped her gaze to the floor. "You know I'd appreciate whatever you can do, Cherry. I'll let you get to it."

"I'll email you when I've got it in order, honey. Expect it by five." Her lips formed a bright pink moue. "And Graydon, you bring that puppy of yours by to say hello next time you have her in the building." She picked up her coffee and took a sip. "It sure is nice knowing our town is in such *capable* hands. Thank you for the delicious surprise."

"Happy to brighten your day, even a little."

"Oh, you do," Cherry said.

Aleja's ears were still hot as she made her way back to the atrium. Graydon didn't stay to flirt more and followed her out.

She shook her head at him. "At least you didn't go super corny and wink at her."

"That was up next." He winked.

It was adorable.

Grrr.

"I can't believe it," she grumbled. "Cookies and logic get nowhere, but forearms and a coffee have me getting my permit by five o'clock?"

He cocked a brow. "Forearms?"

She rolled her eyes. "You flexed on purpose."

"Got you what you need, didn't it?"

"Yes," she said, knowing she was taking her testiness out on the wrong person. "And you can stop smirking about it anytime."

"Don't think I will." He leaned in, sharing-secrets close. Close enough it would take a mere fraction of a movement to brush her lips against his cheek, his mouth. He had the kind of body Aleja could curl up against with abandon, strapping and hard and—

"You're pretty when you're irritated."

Her jaw dropped. "What?"

He paled and backed up a step. "I mean—I *didn't* mean—"

She reached out wildly, and her hand landed on his chest. She couldn't bring herself to pull it back. "No, it's okay. I don't mind the compliment. I'm just not used to hearing it from you."

Glancing down at her splayed fingers, he covered her hand with his wide palm. "I'd give you a thousand compliments a day if you wanted me to."

His eyes were bright, tender. Like waking to a sunny morning full of endless possibilities.

Endless possibilities with Gray Halloran?

Try *not* possible.

"I can't want that, Gray. *We* can't."

His earnestness faded. "I know."

"I said we *couldn't* want it." She leaned closer, her body wanting nothing more than to learn the shape of him. It was ill-advised and complicated and—

And it's the most tempting thing I've felt in a very long time.

"I didn't say I *didn't* want it," she finished.

Which was ridiculous. Why the hell was she even entertaining a kiss with someone as complicated as Graydon?

Satisfaction teased the corners of his mouth and his gaze flicked over her shoulder, around the empty lobby and at the receptionist who walked away from her desk and into a back room. "Bear with me for a second."

"Huh?"

"Just—" his hand slid to cup her neck "—one second. Okay?"

Her breath hitched. They were in public. Someone they knew could walk through the lobby doors at any moment. She should back away. But what would one second hurt? "One small kiss."

His lips molded against hers in a fleeting butterfly touch. Too short to be anything, really.

But the glow flooding her veins, the sparks on her lips and the urge to reach for more?

Not exactly nothing.

Her heart raced. She rose on her toes to deepen the kiss, but he stepped back.

"Only a small one, right?" he said, expression glazed.

"Yeah, small. Of course." He'd caught her trying to get closer. Trying to get more. Would he take it the wrong way? Assume she was interested?

Are you sure you're not?

A gust of air from the opening automatic door nipped her blazing cheeks. Had someone seen—

The person who walked through the door wasn't anyone she knew.

Phew. Her smile wobbled. "Yeah. No big deal."

"Right. We'll go with that." He ran a thumb along her cheek, eyes twinkling. "For now."

Gray's next two days dragged like they were a month long. Mainly because they were on the weekend, so Aleja wasn't at the lodge. He worked all Monday and missed cruising by the project to check to see if she'd gotten her permits and to see if the delayed drywall had arrived. He'd intended to go by this morning, but *I'll lie down for an hour* had turned into four. Good thing he'd told Emma he needed the morning off to catch up on sleep after his rotation.

It'd been a quiet shift, filled with menial chores around the station. Gave him plenty of time to think, and he had plenty to think about.

Mainly seven little words: *I didn't say I didn't want it.*

The double negative hadn't distracted him from the meaning.

She liked it when he complimented her.

And she'd liked it when he kissed her, however briefly. Her reaction after the fact, telling him it was no big deal, had been bluster.

Did he have a shot at another kiss?

He hadn't lied about not wanting to be on the market. Playing the field, dating his way through the eligible and interested women in Sutter Creek? Nah.

The few times he'd tried something casual or had gone on a date lacking any immediate connection, he'd walked away feeling unfulfilled, hollow. He'd learned to accept his internal wiring, that he needed to see the potential for forever with a woman before he dated her. Meant his relationship experience was limited to one long-term high school girlfriend and a college relationship that had lasted for most of his sophomore and junior years. The side bonus of knowing he wasn't emotionally up for casual dating was avoiding adding yet another page to the *Gray Can't Take Anything Seriously* book his family had been writing since his birth.

Only one woman interested him right now, and she wasn't interested in dating, for "obvious reasons."

Which—fair enough. Maybe she didn't think anyone would want to take on a new relationship with someone who was about to become a parent to twins. Or maybe it was connected to her last relationship. He'd been in his first year of college, so he'd missed the drama, but Nora had mentioned enough for him to learn Aleja had broken things off with her fiancé not long before they were supposed to get married.

Curiosity teased, and he fought with his tangled comforter.

He wasn't about to try to convince her that she should want a relationship. Her reasons were her own, and were valid, whatever they were.

But he really wanted to know *what* they were.

Because for the first time in his life, he sensed they might have a real connection.

Maybe an actual chance.

"Hell," he said to Penny, who was spinning in hitching, three-legged circles beside his bed, trying to catch her long, thin tail. "How is that new? I've always wanted to know what makes her tick."

Penny plopped on her rear and cocked her head.

"Oh, you think that would work? If you stared at her with those cute eyes, she'd spill her secrets?"

The puppy whined.

"Can't hurt to try. I sure can't say no to you. Maybe Aleja will be the same."

He took twenty minutes to wash off any post-nap funk and pick a pair of jeans and a flannel shirt that looked nice enough without making it obvious he was trying to look nice.

Checking his phone and confirming the time—a few minutes until eleven—he tucked Penny inside the modified baby carrier she was almost getting too big for and sneaked down the back set of stairs to the hallway separating the kitchen from the dining hall.

He managed to flag down one of the waitstaff, who agreed to put together a plate of cheese, crackers and fruit for him.

Rather, the waitress got sucked into *Penny's* irresistible brown gaze, softening her up enough that she didn't seem to mind giving Gray a hand.

"See?" he said to Penny once the waitress left them to fulfill the favor. He scratched behind one of the dog's ears, earning a nibble on the chin. "No one can hold up under your charms."

"I can." A beleaguered voice came from behind him.

He groaned and turned to face his sister.

"What's with the animal in my kitchen?"

"I'm not in the kitchen. I'm in the hall."

"If a food inspector showed up, I don't think they'd care about the nuance." She stepped closer and touched her nose to Penny's. "I'm sorry Auntie Emma needs to be a meanie. It's not your fault your dad doesn't know how to follow basic rules."

The waitress brought out the platter, and Gray thanked her.

"What, and free food, too?" she teased.

His neck heated. "It's not for me."

Emma cocked an eyebrow. "Oh? Interesting."

"Plus, you know I'm paying for any meals I eat."

"And for meals *not* for you."

"Yeah, uh, I'd better go. Wouldn't want to break your rules for any longer than necessary."

He headed for the exterior door connected to the shortest path to the construction entrance.

She followed him down the hall. "Imagine what fourteen-year-old you would have thought, seeing this much of Aleja."

A lifetime of get-ready-for-some-sister-torture conditioning tickled his neck. "Probably would have questioned my sanity for giving up most of my days off to be your lackey."

"As if. You looked for any excuse to be around her when you were that age."

"A high school kid with a crush," he admitted. No point in hiding it, and maybe in creating a solid line between then and now, he'd be able to keep his current feelings far away from his sister's perceptive gaze.

"And now?"

"What about now?"

She smirked. "You're still moony-eyed."

Damn it. He felt like he was a deer walking through the woods. Any sudden movement, any too-strong defensiveness or some of the sarcasm threatening to bubble up, and Emma would pull the trigger. "Have I been wearing the same lovesick expression Luke's had on?"

Her gaze went soft. "Does he? Look lovesick, that is?"

Sister distracted? Check. "He stares at you like you're a fish-laden riffle on a river. The source of all his happiness." His high-heel-and-dress-loving sister's engagement to someone with a serious fly-fishing habit was causing no end of ribbing from their family.

The Hallorans—showing love by giving each other a hard time. Innocent, in the case of Emma and Luke.

It hadn't always been for Gray.

All things considered, Emma teasing him about Aleja was a thousand times more preferable to being referred to as The Big Oops or Oopsie for most of his junior year of high school. Those words clung to a guy, long after they were said.

They parted ways at the doorway, with Luke juggling the plate far away from his body to avoid Penny's highly motivated tongue.

By the time he got to the construction tent, he'd almost dropped the food twice.

One of Aleja's carpenters, a thirtysomething guy who went to Gray's mom's church, was busy at the band saw. His twin daughters were in Emma's Brownie troop, too.

"Darren, man, is the boss around?" Gray asked.

The carpenter paused and wiped some sawdust from a dark brown cheek. "She's gone into Bozeman this morning."

"Oh." He feigned a no-biggie reaction. "Guess I'll come back later."

He could put the food in his fridge. Didn't solve his need to see Aleja's smile and appease his curiosity about her reasons for avoiding relationships. There had to be a reason why she'd been alone for so long.

The other man smiled. "Nice baby you have there."

Gray grinned. "She's not going to tolerate being bundled much longer, but it's been convenient while she's still so small."

"Might be time to get yourself a human baby, then," Darren said.

He did a double take. Both at the casual suggestion he could handle being a father and the actual thought of having a child. It didn't take much effort to picture having a kid strapped to his chest instead of a puppy. "Maybe one day. And if you see Aleja, let her know I'm looking for her. I owe her a snack."

Chapter Eight

"See, I told you it was normal for your belly to be measuring ahead."

In true Nora style, the reassurance was delivered in an all-knowing tone. Aleja supposed she deserved it. She'd been fretting all week, getting sucked into random advice and opinions on pregnancy website message boards.

"Lesson learned. Walk away from the computer," Aleja said.

She should have walked away from Gray, too. Instead, she'd kissed her best friend's brother in the entrance to city hall. Yeah, they'd been alone in the front atrium, but it was still a miracle no one had noticed. She'd been waiting all week for Nora to find out. But they'd made it to Bozeman and back without any hint of a *You did what with my little brother?* challenge, so she was pretty sure she was safe.

Keep telling yourself that.

She groaned silently. Truth. One tiny kiss from Gray and she'd been lit on fire.

Nora steered her truck along the highway that followed the Gallatin River to the turnoff for Sutter Creek, and Sutter Mountain beyond it. Aleja would have driven to her own appointment, but Nora had insisted on coming, and on driving since she got carsick as a passenger.

"I knew I'd get a bump earlier," Aleja said, stretching out in the passenger seat, enjoying the familiar view of snow-dusted trees and the winding, ice-edged river. "But it's still weird. Feels so fast. I'm used to having curves, but not like this. And definitely not like it'll be toward the end."

If a single pregnancy was like a basketball, would a twin belly be like a beach ball? Hard to imagine. She put her hands on her twelve-week bump. It was as round as she'd be at seventeen weeks with one baby, according to the doctor. She'd unmistakably popped. She was starting to notice it while bending over at work, though Dr. Lopez had assured her she was still safe to do anything that felt comfortable.

She and Nora had stopped in at a maternity store, where she'd loaded up on jeans and shirts with more give to them. Tired of not being able to button her pants, she'd worn a pair of the stretch-waisted, under-the-stomach jeans out of the store. It was a hundred percent more comfortable.

Also a hundred percent more obvious.

"The sprouts aren't in the mood to be private anymore. It's time to tell my crew. A Valentine's Day surprise for them." God, she was nervous. How would they react? "Do you think they'll doubt my ability to finish the job? I have no time to deal with pushback."

"Your crew is made up of good people. If anything, they'll try to help you too much."

"Hopefully they don't feel lied to."

"No one's entitled to your personal information."

"Maybe everyone will be like your brother," Aleja said. "He seems unfazed."

"Yeah?" Nora tapped the steering wheel a few times. "Not like it has much to do with him, though. He's not as invested as people who have their businesses on the line."

"He's not, but…"

After a few seconds, Nora said, "But what?"

"He cares about the lodge. About the familial connection. He's determined to make sure he doesn't owe Emma anything, and he's been working hard on whatever tasks she gives him. So I imagine he cares about the renos, too."

Nora's brows furrowed. "He should have moved back home to Mom and Dad's once he lost his apartment. Then he could have been on-site to pitch in with ranch work when we need him. Emma's just being kind, putting him up at the lodge. Instead, it's 'Emma needs…' this, and 'my shift went long' that, and 'my puppy' this, and 'paramedic training' that…"

Irritation rose on Gray's behalf. "That's his passion, Norie. His career. *You* put the ranch first, but it's your job. And he's doing his."

Nora frowned. "At least one of my siblings was supposed to help me carry the load. Gray seemed the most likely. Emma always wanted to do her own thing, and Bea has the vocational attention span of a gnat."

"Why not Jack?" The Hallorans' cousin, who was a year younger than Nora and Aleja, had lived with them at the RG Ranch for most of elementary school and all of high school.

"He fell in love with fighting fire."

"And Gray's not allowed to do the same?"

An epic scowl crossed Nora's face. "Whose side are you on? Has he somehow pulled you in with that golden-boy charm?"

Her face heated. "You and I are biased toward helping out with our respective family businesses because it's what we both do. And even though I picked construction with my dad instead of following in Grandpa Joe and my mom's footsteps, I see what ranching takes out of Rafael. I know it's the same for you. But I'd be pissed off if he treated my choice as less worthy than his. Did you feel obligated to work for the RG?"

"No, I chose it."

"And it would have been equally valid *not* to choose it. Like Gray did."

"I guess," Nora grumbled. "I still don't know why you're defending my brother so hard."

"He's a good guy." *Man. A good* man.

One I might want to kiss again.

Nora all but rolled her eyes before asking, "Enough about Gray. What's your plan?"

"Well, definitely not to inconvenience you by getting you to play taxi service too often. I'm glad for the company, but I'm sure the steers are annoyed you've deserted them."

"The steers can live without me for a morning. I don't want you to be alone for your appointments."

"Well, there are going to be a lot of them."

"You just had to do something special." Nora's teasing smile faltered.

"What's that look for?"

Nora reached over and laid her hand on Aleja's bump. "I'm envious."

"You could be a single mom if you wanted."

Nora shook her head and put her hand back on the wheel. "I'm not cut out for that. But you're going to be amazing."

"I hope so. At least I've had a lot of practice with my nieces and nephews. And my twins aren't going to be much younger than Bree's baby." Her sister's child wasn't a year old yet. "Even Rafa's youngest, for that matter."

The mention of her brother earned a frown.

Aleja snorted. One of these days, Rafael and Nora would stop sniping at each other long enough to realize they clashed because they were two peas in a pod. "If you don't want to be a single parent, then find someone to have a kid with."

"Keep dreaming, dreamer."

"I will. What's life without dreaming?" It was what pushed her at work and had driven her to be a mom.

"So, you'd nudge me to find love, but won't look for it yourself?"

Aleja patted her stomach. "You don't have my baggage."

"That's not your baggage."

"What do you mean?"

Nora bit her lip and sighed. "You're afraid of risk."

"Having *twins* isn't taking a risk?"

"Not one that requires trusting a partner, no," Nora said quietly. "Ever since Trace—"

"This is not about Trace. This is about me not finding a partner *since* Trace, and not wanting to wait to have a family any longer. As if I'd suppress hurt feelings for over seven years."

"I'm just saying, there were a lot of hurt feelings to suppress." Nora's voice was feather-gentle.

"I'm glad I found out what I did. Had we gotten married and then I found out he'd lied about wanting to have kids? Way worse. It was a blessing."

"And blessings hurt sometimes."

Aleja closed her eyes, trying to force out the echo of the humiliation of premarital counseling. Of Trace admitting to Father Flanigan—of course, it had to be in front of Abuela's favorite priest—that he didn't want to have kids. Of Rafael, fresh off a divorce, taking out some of his own relationship issues out on Trace.

The two nearly coming to blows on Main Street had set gossip infernos all over Sutter Creek. As had the severed friendship between her parents and Trace's. Her parents had been livid when their life-long friends had talked all over town about how they thought Aleja should surrender her dream of having children.

"Yeah, it did hurt me. My family, too. But it's not why I'm not seeing anyone now."

"Okay, hon."

That doubtful tone… *Argh.* Since when did her best friend not trust Aleja to know what was best for her life? "I'm going to rock doing this by myself. My business will be *fine.* My *babies* will be fine."

As long as I stop tempting myself with your damn brother.

Of course, he was the first person she saw when she got to the lodge. Approaching via the outside path, she couldn't miss him, crouched down working on a command with his puppy. His shoulders were impossibly broad in his canvas jacket. And the way those jeans were cupping his ass? Delicious.

He moved with the ease of a man who'd been working with animals all his life. The ranch might not be his passion like Nora wished it would be, but he had enough experience to look like a natural.

Competence was the sexiest thing.

And the taste of his lips, the way he held a woman with care and control—

Also sexy. *Damn.*

He stood and turned, as if he'd sensed her presence. His smile hit her full force, unrestrained and genuine. She couldn't remember the last time a man had greeted her with so much joy, every time.

Is he a Labrador in a human body, or is he saving them up for me?

She loved it.

It scared the bejeezus out of her.

Especially when his eyes were not only smiling but flicking down her body. Covert, but obviously checking her out.

"I had to get new jeans," she blurted, coming closer to ensure no one would hear the conversation if they happened to walk by. Close enough she could smell his warm, masculine scent through the bite of snow and evergreens.

"They look..." His pupils flared. "Nice."

"They look like maternity jeans," she murmured.

"Maternity jeans can't look nice?"

"I didn't expect them to."

"You expected wrong." His words were gruff. "You look more than nice, Aleja. Try beautiful."

She couldn't stop her eyes from widening. "I thought you weren't going to say stuff like that."

He held her gaze, strong, insistent. "But then you admitted you liked it."

"It's not smart."

"But it makes you smile," he said, leaning in a little closer.

"I can't go there, Gray. Not even harmless flirting."

"Why not?"

"Uh, the babies?"

He paused. His throat bobbed. "And what if the babies aren't a no-go for me?"

"How can you possibly know that?"

"How can you be so sure you know what I think?"

She choked out a laugh. "No guy's going to want to take on twins."

"I disagree," he said. "How did your appointment go?"

She pulled out the newest ultrasound picture. One bonus to carrying two babies—she got to see them on-screen more often. "They're still growing."

Wonder crossed his face. He took the small image from her. "Wow, it even shows their hands."

"Hands. Feet. Stubborn Flores chins. And next month, I'll get to find out their biological sexes."

"Right, they're not identical."

"That a baby scan, Aleja?" Her plumber's voice came from behind them. "Did the kid here knock you up?"

Alejandra snatched the photo back from Gray and jammed it in her pocket. She whirled to face Vern, a man in his fifties who Aleja didn't like much, but sometimes had to take on as a subcontractor due to a lack of other plumbers in the area. "Excuse me?"

"Thought you were getting a little chubby," Vern said.

Aleja's cheeks went radioactive hot. "Again, excuse me?"

"Christ, man. In what world is it okay to be so disrespectful?" Gray said.

She appreciated the support, but she could handle this herself. She fixed Vern with a stern look. "I'm going to give you one free pass, because I'm in a good mood. Yes, I'm pregnant. Twins, in fact. Not Graydon's. It won't affect the project. And anyone who says anything less than professional on my job site will be asked to leave, so I expect you to do better." She stalked past him. "Excuse me. I should tell everyone before they find out from someone else."

She stalked through the outer doors into the almost completed basement great room. It smelled like floor wax and low-VOC paint. Emma choosing environmentally friendly options was a bonus for Aleja—fewer substances she had to worry about working around.

She got the crew's attention and waved them in. As they gathered, she admired the progress. "Looking good this morning. Let's chat for a few before we break for lunch."

Murmurs met her, and a few drifting gazes.

Saving everyone the trouble of wondering, she splayed her fingers over her bump. "Last year, I decided to become a mom. I'm twelve weeks pregnant. Turns out I'm having twins."

Her electrician let out a low whistle.

Darren grinned. "Congratulations. You're in for a ride."

"Thanks. I plan to hit you up for advice, given you're a heck of a father to your girls."

Not everyone looked as excited for her. The other four crew members were wearing expressions ranging from worried to downright angry.

Vern stomped back inside, with Gray on his heels. Why he felt the need to follow, she didn't know, but his calm presence made it easier to lift her chin and stare down the plumber.

And hoo-boy, was Vern spitting mad. "How can you tell us this'll go to plan? This project has our names on the line, too."

Darren cleared his throat. "I think what Vern means to say is, you're our leader, and we don't want you to get hurt."

"I'll be careful, as always. People can be pregnant and do physical jobs."

"Jennifer Jones was on shift with me until she was seven months along," Gray said. "And firefighting is a hell of a lot more dangerous than construction work."

"Beg to disagree with you, Gray," her electrician interjected. "This work can be mighty dangerous, and JJ is a freaking wonder. She's a good friend of mine. And she's so tall she was barely showing at seven months. No offense, Aleja, but you already look pregnant."

Darren looked thoughtful. His earlier smile was long gone. "It's a good point. When my wife was carrying our twins, she needed me to put on her shoes for the last couple of months."

Aleja put her hands on her hips. "I get it—this is

an unusual situation. And I don't expect to be working past June. Which means work, work, work now. This is going to be my one hundred percent focus until I have to go on maternity leave."

"The complete overhaul, plus the cabin, in three months?"

"And twelve days."

Darren whistled.

She held up a hand. "The cabin will be completed without me being hands-on. But the lodge will get done."

She had far too many plans to leave the details work to someone else.

Discontented mumbles filled her ears.

"Hey." She waved a hand around the basement area, nearly transformed into a multipurpose space that would be styled as a cozy café. Wood and glass walls, slate floors and cushy, spend-a-day-with-a-book couches. Aleja smiled just thinking of the preliminary sketches of the furnished room. "Look at what we've done already. We'll be working on the facade and service bar by the weekend. It'll be time to move upstairs before we know it. I promise."

"Are you going to step aside early if you need to?" Darren asked cautiously.

"If I have to. But I'll oversee it to the end. The only thing more important than my vision and our project is bringing my babies safely into the world."

Her crew didn't look convinced. *Sigh.* Well, the best way to convince them was to show them.

"Let's get to work," she said.

There was a whole lot of muttering, but people followed her lead.

"Aleja," Gray said, arms full of zonked-out puppy. "Do you have a second? I've got something for you."

"I have a lot to get crossed off the list today. Can it wait?"

The corners of his mouth turned down. "Yeah, sure. I'll come back later."

Penny snuffled.

Aleja's heart squished. "I think I need a kiss first."

"You said you only wanted one," Gray murmured.

"I meant from the puppy!" She cupped the sides of the dog's head and buried her burning face in the loose, velvet-soft fur between Penny's ears. "Obviously."

"Yeah, obviously." His voice rasped. "I'll come find you later."

He strode away.

Later. Okay. Fine.

So long as *later* didn't involve another kiss.

"Oh, you want to come say hi to Aleja, too?" Gray asked his dog, figuring it was time to call it quits on his maintenance shift for the day. The entire lodge smelled like the Valentine's Day buffet being served in the dining room, and he was starting to drool worse than Penny did when presented with a few kernels of buttered popcorn.

She whined from inside her portable dog pen. No

one needed his puppy creating havoc while doing inventory on the fishing gear in the tackle room.

Gray laughed at her attempt to sit pretty, with her one front paw planted, her shorter leg raised and her head cocked. "Ten weeks old and you've got me figured out. Fine. Let's call it a day."

He disassembled the pen and fixed her in her harness and leash. "I know. You like the lovely lady, too. Probably not as much as I do, but I agree, she's great."

An opinion only affirmed when, snacks in hand, he found Aleja looking gorgeous as she swore at the linoleum she was stripping off one of the side staircases. Dark eyes, assessing and smart. Silky pieces of hair escaping from her ponytail. Filthy words escaping from between those plush lips.

He chuckled at the jumbled combination of Spanish and English. It reminded him of his Spanish classes in high school and college—like any kid, he'd learned the profanity first.

"Who would put linoleum on a staircase, anyway?" he asked.

"Either one of your grandparents or Hank Emerson," she said ruefully, rocking back on her heels. "Whoever owned the place back in—" she held up a piece of linoleum "—1974?"

"That would've been Gramps or Grammy." Holding Penny in one arm to keep her safe from nails and other hazards, he held out the plate of food he'd been saving in his fridge. "I wanted to give you this earlier, the elevenses I promised you. But it'll still be delicious."

"Five-thirtieses?" she asked.

He laughed. "Hobbits eat dinner at six, if I have it right. And supper is at nine p.m. Though I'm not sure that's canon. Nora read me the books when I was little, and I can't remember if mealtimes were mentioned in the actual text."

A smile flirted with her mouth. "Nerd."

"Guilty."

She peered at the plate, gratitude brightening her expression. "How did you know I'd be ravenous?"

"Good guess. Looks like you need company, too."

She sighed. "I sent my crew home, but I want to get the staircase stripped."

He chuckled. "I could give you a hand."

"I won't say no." She pointed at the array of cheeses, meats and fruit. "I'm going to eat that first, though."

"I was hoping you would."

She squinted. "The gouda is heart-shaped."

"For Valentine's Day, I guess. Emma has a whole banquet going on tonight."

"Oh, geez, I keep forgetting the date."

Huh. If he were her boyfriend, he'd spoil her so badly she'd never forget it was a day dedicated to romance. Waffles in bed. Snuggling on the couch with silly comedies all day. A twilight snowshoe on the mountain followed by all the tapas they could eat at the upscale bar in the lodge at the top of the

Peak Chair. And a night filled with sending her to the stars and back.

This evening, he'd have to settle for feeding her some charcuterie. He jerked his head toward the main floor. "Come on. Taking a half hour for dinner won't kill you."

"I—" An entire argument took place on her face within three seconds. If he had to guess, it was "I do not want to share a meal with my best friend's little brother on Valentine's Day," countered with, "but I'm hungry," then, "I don't want to give him the wrong idea," followed by, "but I'm really, really hungry."

"Yes? No?" he said.

"Not sure I'm in the mood to eat on a sawhorse, but I'm way too dusty to eat in the dining room with a bunch of people celebrating Valentine's Day."

"You're welcome to my kitchen table. It's small, but it works for two."

The possibilities of having Aleja alone in his space were endless, but sharing a meal with her was more than he would have expected a few weeks ago. He'd start there and see where it went.

Aleja leaned back in her chair and groaned with joy, settling her hands on her belly. Not because of the babies, but because she was full of cheese, one of the three best states of being—number one being busy in her garage workshop and number two being curled under a blanket.

Being curled under a blanket next to a hulking firefighter?

She didn't want to like that idea, but she did.

She didn't want to like the hungry look on his face, either.

But I do.

"I came here for cheese," she blurted, needing to clarify for herself as much as him. "Not because it's Valentine's Day. Or because of what happened at city hall."

His lips quirked and he lounged back in his chair, opposite her across the small round table. "What part of what happened at city hall?"

"Kissing."

Amusement shifted into a full-on grin. "So, it's been on your mind, then."

"Of course, it has been. You're my best friend's little brother, and I kissed you. *In a public place.*"

"And you liked it."

Dios mío, the man looked satisfied.

She lifted a brow. "You're missing the point."

"Am I?"

Ugh. She didn't know anymore. She dropped her head back and stared at the hideous popcorn ceiling—she'd smooth that out the minute she got the chance—so when he spoke, it was just his words flowing over her. Not his infernal, addictive smile.

"Nora's the reason for your hesitation? And me being younger than you?"

"Yes," she said. *Liar. Be honest.* "Argh, fine. No.

That's something to handle delicately, but it wouldn't be a never-going-to-happen. I think your family would be respectful if we were both willing to have a serious relationship."

"And we're not?"

"*I'm* not. I'm having twins. I have a million-dollar renovation on the go. I don't have time for anything other than work and preparing to be a mom."

"And eating cheese," he said.

Was he joking as a defense mechanism? Maybe to make her laugh...

"Well, cheese is a basic life necessity," she said.

"So's kissing."

"Not for me, not right now. Nor do I think you've put enough time into thinking about the reality of being in a relationship with someone preparing to be a single parent to brand-new babies."

He narrowed his eyes for a second before taking a deep breath and nodding. "I'm not going to push you for something you don't want to give."

"I appreciate that." At his core, Graydon was a decent human being.

"I'm also not going to say no to spending time together when it fits," he continued. "I enjoy your company. And your lips. Both the words that come out of them and the way they feel on mine."

"*Gray.*"

He shrugged. "Just being honest."

"*Alarmingly* so."

"Maybe, but you deserve nothing less than the facts."

Oh. Did he know how much she prized truthfulness? She averted her gaze, at a loss for how to respond.

His dog, who was across the room attacking a rubber river otter toy and looking precious, abandoned her battle and trotted over to Gray. She licked his hand, which hung at his side. He cupped her round little belly and lifted her to his chest. Penny settled in with a satisfied sigh.

Made sense. Who wouldn't want to nuzzle against Gray's rock-solid pecs?

People with their priorities in order.

Aleja jolted to her feet.

Too fast—her head spun, and she grabbed the back of the chair.

Gray was at her side in a second. A band of strong, sinewy muscle wrapped around her shoulders.

"I'm not going to faint," she said, vision still shadowy. "I'm just dizzy."

The puppy wiggled in the crook of his other elbow, but he held both Aleja and Penny steady. "Take a breath. Four seconds in, eight out."

Aleja followed instructions.

Her vision sharpened. So did all her senses. Seeing, smelling, feeling—it was all Gray. His flannel shirt brushing the back of her neck and the tang of his lime-scented soap and the concern stealing the light from his blue eyes.

"I'm okay. Promise," she whispered.

And she'd be more okay if she got to taste him, too. The man made a good point about kissing being a life necessity. Tilting her face to his, she pressed her lips to his jaw.

Chapter Nine

Damn, how was Gray supposed to be halfway logical with Aleja's lips on his skin? Her disheveled, end-of-the-workday ponytail, along with her sexy new jeans and the T-shirt pulling tight across her full breasts, made it impossible to think.

Tightening his arm around her shoulders, he took a breath. Then he put the dog down. If luck went his way, he'd need both hands for what came next. "As much as I love being close, I want to make sure I'm reading you correctly."

Her hand landed on his cheek, directing his face closer to her mouth. His body tightened, craving another sip of her. "I'm conceding the point that a few secret kisses won't be anything except a good time."

"Are you saying that because it's Valentine's Day?"

"Would it matter if I was?"

"No," he said. "I'm good for a few kisses, whenever and wherever."

Yeah, he preferred to have more certainty at the beginning of a relationship. But even if she didn't see the long-term possibilities yet, he did. And she was the kind of woman a man went all in on, even if all he had was a pair of twos.

"And we'll keep it between us?"

Fighting the disappointment at her limitations, he wove his fingers into the escaping curls on either side of her head. "Whatever you need."

Her gaze softened.

Enough waiting. He lowered his mouth to hers. Tasted her, slow at first. The sweetness of the fruit she'd eaten with the cheese, mixed with something uniquely her. A delight he'd only gotten a hint of before.

But now? Now they had time, and privacy.

He could devour her like he'd always dreamed. He lowered a hand, pressed it against the curve of her back, bringing the softness of her breasts and her belly flush against his stomach, his length.

She growled a needy complaint, nipping at his lips, eyes wide with heat and something he sure as hell hoped was craving.

Did she feel this as much as he did? Did she share his desire to lose himself in her, to take her with him?

"I need to get downstairs." A weak protest, at best.

"Finish ridding the world of the linoleum abomination."

He used another long kiss to disagree.

The taste of her was intoxicating. Need blurred the edges between her and him, between logic and lust.

"If I promise to come help you," he said, "would you stay longer?"

She rose on her toes again, a wordless, yearning answer. Her hips shifted along his front, seeking, not quite reaching. Her bump was full enough to make the angle tricky.

Weeks ago, he never would have thought he'd find that a turn-on, but he shouldn't have been surprised. Everything about Aleja made him hungry for more.

Guiding her backward, he sat on the edge of the bed and tugged her hand, coaxing her toward him, spreading his knees to get her closer. "C'mere."

Her legs bumped the edge of the bed, but she didn't climb on. "But…"

He stilled, waited, cocking an eyebrow.

She bit her lip, smoothed her shirt down her front. Her gaze dropped to his lap.

Waiting for her to decide her next move, he clutched the comforter.

"I *should* leave," she whispered.

A flicker of hope burned low, lit by her inflection. "Yeah?"

"Mmm-hmm." Those lips, humming a soundtrack to whatever mental battle was clashing in her mind. He hadn't even scratched the surface of enjoying them.

Swallowing, he slid his palms along smooth, denim-clad thighs, stopping right before the curve of her bottom.

She whimpered. "I should go downstairs and finish my work and not..."

"Not enjoy each other?" His voice was raw. Good. The clearer she could see the effect she had on him, the better. A flick of a button and a zipper and he'd be able to lean in and kiss away her doubts. Bury his tongue in her heat. Make her dissolve.

"I've never pictured this happening," she said, glancing away.

He'd imagined it enough for both of them. And he knew she was lying. "Never?"

A rosy bloom broke across her cheeks. "Maybe."

"I didn't invite you here for a hookup. But it seems like a hell of an idea."

"Maybe," she repeated. Her hand drifted to her abdomen, fingers spreading starfish-wide, as if to secret away what had to be some unreal changes to experience. "But—"

"Don't worry about that."

Her nervous smile suggested she was. "To be clear, you mean sex?"

"I mean pleasure." He leaned in, kissing the back of the hand resting over her navel. "Yours. Mine."

"Mmm, vague, then."

If she asked, he'd have to admit he didn't have a ton of experience beyond oral. His high school girlfriend hadn't believed in sex before marriage, and he'd respected her decision. In college, both he and his girlfriend had been paranoid of her getting pregnant. The last thing he'd wanted was to have a child who eventually discovered they were unplanned. Needless to say, he'd gotten a hell of a lot of practice with his tongue and fingers.

"You want specific? There's nothing more I want than to make you come." He feathered his thumbs along the seams of her jeans' pockets. "I'm a curious man. I want to learn how you taste, how you feel. What your eyes look like when they're glazed and satisfied."

She arched closer, and he grinned.

"I want to take your mind off things." He teased the edge of her T-shirt up. His fingertips met the warm, smooth skin of the small of her back. He lingered there, savoring the chance to touch her in a place he never imagined he would. Innocent, yet not.

"What makes you think I need a distraction?"

"Think? Nah. I know it."

Challenge sparked in her eyes. "Really."

Cocky kid, in other words.

"Let me show you. Just for a night."

Just one night?

That was a cliché that belonged in one of her sister Josefina's telenovelas. Not something to share with Gray Halloran.

And yet, he wasn't alone in his curiosity. His words and promises shimmied along her skin, pulling her toward forbidden temptation. For an expert at putting out fires, he sure knew how to light them with his fingertips.

She was running out of excuses, out of reasons to ignore the sparks charging the air between them. His playful smile twitched as he leaned back a little, hands planted and arms straight, his built torso on display, the angle saying *I'm here. Yours, if you want me.*

And she did. The absurdity of wanting him had come from nowhere, but it wasn't going anywhere.

The buttons on his shirt beckoned to be opened. Her fingers fumbled, dancing across crisp cotton and the widening V of hair-dusted skin. Desire built, a slow shimmy along her limbs. Her newfound companion, and she'd been fighting it.

Why, though? Giving in would feel so much better. Her body craved pressure, a hard, hot man to envelop her—

Not any man. This man.

She put a hand to his bare chest and knelt one knee on the outside of a thick thigh. "We say goodbye in a few hours and forget this happened?"

Disappointment darkened his eyes, a deep, stormy cobalt. "Forget? I can't promise that. You're not the kind of woman I can put out of my mind." His throat bobbed and his palms stilled on her back. "I won't expect more from you, though."

She straddled him, rocking forward, melting at the granite heat behind his fly. Every nerve ending rubbed against denim and his erection. Bliss flooded her with each shift and slide. Humming her satisfaction, she kissed him.

He met the gentle touch, a brief span of time where the world narrowed down to the brush of his lips on hers and the softness of his open shirt against her palms, handfuls of cotton in her fists.

"I can't hold you this way," he complained, feathering kisses along her jaw. "I—"

He straightened, cupping her ass. She gripped his shoulders and braced for him to stand or spin around.

"Aleja." His voice was melted sugar and promises. "If you think I'm going to be anything less than gentle with you, you don't know me."

"Don't be gentle, Gray. Not tonight." She wasn't here for a long night of pleasure. "This is just an interlude before we go deal with the rest of the lino from hell. A nooner, evening version."

Firm lips trickled kisses down her neck to her collarbone. Callused fingers tugged the neck of her shirt aside to taste along her shoulder. "All right, then, expediency it is."

He lifted her shirt off and dropped it on the floor. Cool air tickled the skin of her stomach and back. Her head spun. How was this man stripping off her clothes reality?

A low, reverent groan rumbled from his chest. "I've always thought you were gorgeous, but this…"

One wide palm cupped a tender breast through the brand-new, soft-as-air bra she'd splurged on.

She arched against him, settled into the brilliant

touch, until his thumb brushed her nipple. She almost launched off the bed. "Ahh—it's too much, there."

He responded right away, swearing an apology and withdrawing his hand. "I should have asked if you wanted that."

"Mmm, want it? I do. I usually love having my nipples touched. But they're way more sensitive than I'm used to, and you're the first person to go testing it out."

His mouth tipped at one corner. "Let's try something different, then."

Her world tilted as he brought her from his lap to the mattress with careful hands. The navy comforter, not the lodge-standard beige stripes she'd seen while touring the rooms to be renovated, was the softest flannel. He settled her hips on the edge of the bed, her knees bent, toes not quite touching the floor.

"What—" She rose on her elbows to see where he'd gone. He knelt on the floor, expression hungry and heavy-lidded. Damn, those eyes were something… *"Oh."*

"Exactly. You're sexy, and I'm the lucky fool who gets to enjoy you." He pressed kisses between her breasts, skipping past her now-rounded abs to the stretchy edge of her jeans. Hooking his fingertips over the fabric waistband, he tugged them off. His mouth trailed lower, slow nips along the edge of her low-cut underwear. Didn't match her bra, but it was at least a newer pair and in good shape because she'd wanted to wear decent ones for her appointment this morning and—

Stop. Stay present. Who knew when she'd next be naked with a man? With Gray...

He knew what he was doing. His tongue, swirling sweet patterns on her mound as he inched her panties down. His thumbs, tracing tempting lines at the tops of her thighs, opening her legs wider with confident hands.

The sheer euphoria on his face, too.

He really wanted her. It aroused in a way she'd never expected.

This was no childhood crush. This was a hot-blooded man who desired her. Wanted to pleasure her. Felt obvious joy in sliding her underwear down to her ankles and burying his face in a place she'd been thinking of in medical terms for months now.

One kiss, one slow lick, and she nearly levitated off the mattress.

Gripping his hair as an anchor, she writhed against the soft bedding.

His thumbs parted her swollen folds, enough for his tongue to peek in and brush her aching nub. He mumbled something, too low for her to catch the words but in the tone of a man caught uttering a fervent prayer of thanks.

Possessive, intimate kisses consumed her. His hint of stubble rasped her inner thighs. Her hips lifted toward the paradise he doled out. No sense of restraint, the reckless abandon of a lover intent on feasting.

A fingertip—no, two, it was too full to be just one—dipped into her slickness. Not a thrust, a slow, stirring pressure.

"Ung," Talk about stealing her words, her thoughts, her everything.

The world distilled down to Gray and the consuming need he was stirring throughout her body. It felt different. Thicker, fuller, wetter, and she didn't know if it was the hormones and changes in her body or some wild effect of him.

Didn't matter.

The flame flickering through her smoldered, built into an inferno.

She was close, so close to the edge. Teetering, her body off balance and pitching like she had one foot on a cliff and one in midair.

"Let go, Aleja. I want to take you there."

With her heels on his muscled shoulders and her hands grasping the comforter, she sank toward the heat of his tongue and the scrape of his whiskers and the tempest of him begging for the chance to give her a release.

A light burst, white and brilliant, then two, then a cascade, a tingling free fall.

Her legs, her arms, they were there, but not. Numb with the fading ecstasy washing through her.

God help her, she was never going to be able to have dinner at the Hallorans' again without thinking about Gray stealing her upstairs and devouring her until she was as limp as the spaghetti his mom liked to serve with her chicken piccata.

"Gray?" she croaked.

He leaned a hip on the mattress, brushing the back

of his hand across his mouth and chin before kissing her cheek. "You good, Alejandra?"

"Mmm-hmm."

"Me, too."

Not going off the thick erection pressing against the outside of her thigh. Lifting a still-tingling, weak hand, she skimmed her palm along his hard obliques toward his button fly.

She shifted onto her side, bringing them belly to belly. His flat, hers curved in a way she would have thought would make things awkward, but somehow hadn't. He'd focused on her satisfaction alone. And satisfied, he had.

"You're not *completely* good," she said. "It's my turn to get you naked and begging. More, even, if you have a condom somewhere."

She cupped him through his jeans and stroked, slow and easy. Enough to earn a guttural plea.

Kissing her temple, he slipped her hand from his jeans. "I can't." He jerked back, face blanching. "I mean, I *can,* but…" A slow stream of air hissed between his lips. "Not now. Not tonight."

She furrowed her brow, staring at him. "Huh?"

Adjusting his jeans, he winced. "I got what I wanted—you, fading into bliss for a few moments. Taking it further—it's more tempting than anything I've ever experienced. I don't think I can go there, though. Not without getting attached."

"But you said just one night—"

"I know. Moving forward, I'll be a friend who happened to kiss you until you came that one time."

A breath shuddered from his strong chest. "Because if I were to have that kind of sex with you, Aleja, joining with you and losing myself there, coming inside you, with you—I can't, not without some commitment. Which I respect you don't want."

"I—" She shook her head in disbelief. "This has never happened to me before."

"Maybe I'm one of a kind."

Yeah, he certainly was.

Chapter Ten

The next morning, Gray was on shift, sitting at the table in the firehouse kitchen and poking at his oatmeal, when a cold jet of water hit him in the face.

"What the hell?" he spluttered, wiping the cold droplets from his cheeks. "You got my textbook wet." He was using his break as double duty, eating and studying one of his paramedic's modules.

"What's got you so bleary-eyed?" his captain, Mark Jacobs, asked from the sink where he was doing dishes. In one hand, he brandished the spray wand like a firehose, threatening to blast Gray a second time. With the other, he tossed Gray a dish towel. "Thought you were single, wouldn't have stayed up late celebrating Valentine's Day."

"I am." Gray scowled, blotting the pages of his

coursework. "And I wasn't. Did some extra renovation work on the lodge last night."

He'd gone to bed at eleven, muscles aching from peeling up ancient linoleum, and then couldn't fall asleep. Spent hours reliving Aleja's shape on his palms, the taste of her on his tongue.

Hell. He'd had a legitimate chance with her last night, and he'd turned her down. What had he been thinking?

Dishes clanked in the sink. "You need to stay sharp, Halloran. I know you're the type to spend your days off working for your family, but if you want that certification, you'll have to prioritize."

His cheeks heated. Why his captain was able to see what he did for his family when those closest to him couldn't, he didn't know. Being *too* close, maybe. Or stuck in past patterns.

Whatever the reason, Jacobs's advice about priorities was solid. "I know. I saw Jack have to make compromises when he was early on with the forest service."

His older cousin had been working as a smoke jumper for long enough that he was employed year-round in Oregon, not seasonally like most wildland firefighters.

"Talk to him, then. He'd best understand what makes your folks tick."

Gray didn't need wisdom concerning his sisters and parents. He knew the score there. He'd forever be the kid, the one who hadn't chosen to work for one of the family businesses. But he'd sure love a listening ear about Aleja, and if he mentioned it to any of his buddies or coworkers, they'd guess who he was talking about in two seconds.

Jack had always been Gray's honorary brother. Gray's parents had adopted him before Gray was born. And unlike Gray, who'd been trying to shed the loose-lips reputation he'd earned back in high school, Jack had always been a locked vault. Specifically, a vault across state borders. Maybe if Gray was vague enough, his cousin wouldn't guess the identity of the woman who'd tied him in knots.

He cleaned up his breakfast and study materials and headed to a corner of the truck bay for some privacy.

He gripped his cell until the plastic case squeaked. Christ. What kind of advice was he expecting? Even if he did decide he could sleep with Aleja without getting attached, she didn't want that.

Somehow, things hadn't been awkward while they finished the work on the staircase. She'd sent him fragmented smiles that stole pieces of his heart, one by one. Said thank you for the help and then dispatched him with a quick kiss to the cheek. If anything, she'd watched him with concern and a little guilt.

She didn't need to feel that way. She didn't owe him anything.

But you owe it to your job not to be distracted.

Got a minute? FaceTime?

He pressed Send on the message to Jack before he could talk himself out of it.

He expected three dots and a return message of *I'm working*, but instead a call notification popped up.

One tapped button and his cousin's face appeared. His short brown hair was sticking up like he'd run a hand through it. A frown flattened his lips and stress creased his tanned forehead. Going off the armoire behind him, Jack was in his bedroom.

"Of all people," Jack grumbled, skipping past any semblance of a hello, "I didn't think you'd be the one to adopt Georgie's cause."

"Huh?" He shot a confused look at the screen. "What does this have to do with Mom?"

The background shifted from the armoire to an abstract painting as Jack sat down. "I assume she conscripted you into calling me? A waste of time, because believe me, you throwing your three years of fighting fires behind a plea to stay home isn't going to work any more than Paisley giving me the silent treatment since she found out I volunteered, or Georgie and all three of your sisters calling me this morning."

It was Gray's turn to run his own hand through his hair. "I don't know what you're talking about." His cheeks heated. "I called for advice about a woman, not about anything to do with volunteering. Volunteering where? And for what?"

"Australia. Fighting the bushfires," Jack grunted. "I fly out tonight. I'm packing." He flashed the camera toward his bed, the comforter covered with neat stacks of clothes.

"Damn, I'll leave you to it." Adrenaline shot through his system. Those fires were no joke. Horrific footage had been playing on the news 24/7 for a month. Jack needed to focus on keeping his ass alive, not on Gray's love life.

His cousin shook his head. "This'll be the last time I get to talk to you for a couple weeks. What's on your mind? Must be something if you're hiding behind the ladder truck. Or some*one*, if it's about a woman. Is Britt back in town?"

"Nah, she's off selling houses in Albuquerque. Like I'd be hung up on someone who dumped me five years ago."

"Never found anyone else, though, so it stands to reason it has something to do with her."

"I've been too busy to find someone new. College. Training." Beyond a couple of hookups that had taught him he was unsatisfied sharing a sexual experience with a woman he didn't feel connected to, he hadn't been in a relationship since his college girlfriend. "You know how it is."

Jack made a face. Something along the lines of *Do I, though?*

"I guess you're not going to buy that excuse, given you've been with Paisley and fighting fires for eons," Gray said.

"Yeah, not my best point of argument at the moment."

"She's mad you're leaving? Or scared?"

"All that. Hurt, too. Now that she has tenure, she's ready to have kids." Jack scrubbed his face with a palm. "I am, too, but it's hard to do in this job. She's not happy about me being gone during the winter in the middle of us trying to get pregnant." His eyes widened. "Don't tell your mom. I don't want to get her hopes up."

"Ha, yeah, she would be overinvested in any promise of grandchildren."

Maybe I'll *be the one to make it happen for her.*

He'd always thought parenthood would be way off for him. It tended to require having a sex life first, and as evidenced by last night, he was still getting in his own way. But what if Aleja wasn't so dead set on not having a relationship right now, and they got together? Stayed together, to the point of him becoming a father figure to her twins? The possibility of it blossomed in his chest. And as for his mom's dreams of grandkids, she would accept Aleja and her twins as family in a hot second. All the Hallorans would.

Or they'd doubt my ability to be responsible enough to be a dad.

He pushed the intrusive thought away. He *was* responsible. If he was offered the chance to be a dad, to parent alongside Aleja, he might very well take that long-shot fantasy and make it his reality. He'd love her children as if they were his own.

But will I get that chance?

"Why the frown?" Jack said. "Oh, right. You called about a girl."

"She's not a girl," Gray said quietly.

"Who is she?"

"Doesn't matter. It isn't going anywhere."

"Unrequited love. Damn," Jack said.

"Yeah." Generalized sympathy eased the ache, at least. Gray wasn't the first person to want more of a relationship than another person was able to give.

A mug filled most of the screen, Jack taking a sip of whatever he was drinking. "You'll find someone to pop your cherry at some point, kid."

"Jack, I'm not... Britt and I did—"

Jack snorted. "What, like, twice?"

Three times, but who's counting? "Weren't you the one who taught me contraception wasn't failsafe? The last thing I wanted to deal with was an accidental pregnancy in college." No kid needed to know they were an accident, ever. "We did what worked for us. No one went to sleep unhappy." Good grief, why was he explaining this?

"Oh, I remember." Jack's tone was as dry as an empty creek bed. "*Uh...what do girls like, Jack? If you're not, like, going all the way?*"

Gray flipped his cousin the bird. "Do you have to recount that for the entire firehouse?"

"You're the one who called me from work."

"And I'm glad I did, because lack of profound wisdom aside, it's good to talk to you before you head off." Gray was on the verge of saying *be safe,* but Jack was always as careful as possible on the job.

"You want profound? You called the wrong cousin."

"Brother," Gray corrected.

Jack smiled, a little wistful. "Yeah. Brother," he said. "And when it comes to the woman you're interested in? She's allowed her feelings, but so are you.

Not in a force-my-love-on-you kind of way, but you never know when something might change. Listen, be there, be patient. It's the little things." He groaned. "Until it's the big stuff. Look, I'd better finish packing. And see if I can salvage my own relationship before I fly halfway around the world."

They said their goodbyes, and Gray got back to work. *Listen. Be there. Be patient.*

He'd have to be, with Aleja *and* with his own feelings. They'd smoldered for so long, they weren't going to cool off in an instant.

And that's okay.

The best way to show someone love was to meet them where they were. For Aleja, that appeared to be friendship.

Sex, no sex, he was already in love with her. The best way to prove it was to respect her feelings. Last night had been a onetime deal. But it was a Valentine's Day he'd never forget.

You're having twins alone, honey? Aren't you brave?

You're how many weeks? Sixteen? Oof. I would have guessed six months.

Pregnant and working construction? You poor thing.

Aleja stood in the line for Peak Beans, the bustling Main Street coffee shop. She could barely hear the clatter of cups on saucers and the hum of background chatter over the echoes of all the questions she'd faced while doing her banking and prodding Cherry about yet another round of permits.

She needed a coffee like a roofer needed a staple gun. She'd already hit her caffeine limit for the day, but maybe some hot, bitter decaf could fool her brain into thinking it came with an energy boost.

She was two people away from the front of the line when a pair of parka-covered arms wrapped around her from behind.

"Doughnuts for three?" her younger sister Gabriela—Bree to anyone who didn't want a physio dry needle in the eye—said gleefully.

Aleja leaned back into the embrace, happy for the familial support. "No, decaf for one. It's been a morning."

"I bet." Bree shucked the hood of her parka and straightened her short fade cut. "Half my clients have asked about you over the past month. And if I'm getting annoyed by it—which I am—you must be ready to walk around with your fingers in your ears."

"Truth. I should start wearing my safety earmuffs." Joking about the annoyance eased some of the tension in her chest. She knew people were asking because they cared, and because it *was* unusual for someone to be having twins without a partner. "I mean, it's not like I intended to have two babies at once. Nor am I upset over the double blessing."

"Proud of you." Bree's dark brown eyes sparkled.

"If anyone knows what it's like to get questions, it's you," Aleja said. Her sister and her wife had fielded a metric ton of them when they'd conceived.

"Worth it the minute you look into those little baby eyes. And in your case, it'll be twice the joy."

Another parka-clad woman, Bree's boss, Cadie Dawson-Cardenas, sidled up to them. She ran the physical therapy clinic in her family's wellness center. She also happened to be Gray's cousin on his mom's side. Aleja was pretty sure she was tight with Georgie.

What would the two women think if they knew Aleja had hooked up with the youngest Halloran in his makeshift apartment? They might not be bothered at all. *Or* they might be concerned about Gray and Aleja's age difference, or that she was pregnant, or that a messy end could ruin the close ties between their families...

Not that anything had occurred between her and Gray in the month since Valentine's Day. He'd completely respected her wishes, not mentioning their intimacy, not suggesting they follow up with anything romantic. Anytime they'd run into each other at the lodge, they'd kept things congenial. She'd focused on work.

Exactly what she'd asked for.

She was left with the memory of one reckless hour in his apartment.

If only she didn't want so, so much more than that.

"Phew, you're still in line," Cadie said to Bree, putting her hands on her stomach. "I seem to be in the run-to-the-bathroom-every-thirty-minutes stage."

"You're pregnant, too?" Aleja asked.

Cadie nodded. "Took a while—we had to go the same route you did, the fertility clinic in Bozeman. But I'm well over the thirteen-week mark, so I'm hoping we're golden. I'm not sure what Zach and I would have done if I'd had another miscarriage."

Aleja's heart squeezed. "Well, congratulations."

"You, too." Cadie, who looked a lot like Emma and Nora with her long brown hair, smiled at Aleja.

A pang of familiarity ran through her, a flash of being served a similar grin over peeling linoleum. She laughed to herself. Gray must have gotten his smile from the Dawson side of his family.

"Wait, you two have almost identical due dates," Bree said.

Cadie's face brightened even more. "I was thinking of joining the prenatal fitness class my sister's running at the wellness center—want to join me?"

Aleja squashed the knee-jerk *I don't have time* excuse. Getting some exercise would make it easier to stay flexible and to work longer. "I'd love to."

The comfort of a hug from her sister and an invitation from a friend had her so buoyed, she left the coffee shop with her decaf in hand and a full heart, ready to take on one last errand around the corner at the hardware store.

The bell tinkled, and the smell of metal and paint filled her nose. She recognized the back of her dad's head by the cash register. She'd expected he'd be here, had noticed his truck in the lot. He was deep in conversation with the middle-aged owner and her plumber, Vern. Calling out a hello, she headed for the adhesives shelf at the back of the store.

"You gotta be smart, Joe," said the plumber, his not-quite-a-whisper carrying across the store. "She's got another thing coming if she thinks she can finish that project with two babies on the way,"

Aleja froze. Her father's reply was a murmur, indecipherable.

"Who knows what impact it will have on your business after the fact?" Fred, the owner, this time, not bothering to keep his voice down. "She'll be wanting to be a mom, not a contractor. Gonna cut into your bottom line. Delay your retirement."

Aleja gripped the shelf next to her. Her pulse shot into the stratosphere. She wanted to stomp over to the men and tell them to mind their own damn business. Men had children all the time without being questioned about their ability to parent *and* work outside the house. She had dreams for Brooks Contracting that extended beyond her dad's retirement and she planned to make them come true.

She wasn't about to tell the men off now, not when she had tears in her eyes.

The caulking was going to have to wait. Turning on a heel, she hurried from the store to her truck, which she'd parked in the lot between the emergency services side of city hall and Fred's Hardware.

Once ensconced in the driver's seat, she covered her face with her hands and let the tears fall.

I'm not letting my dad down. I'm not.

No matter how many times she repeated it, the sobs came harder.

She went to reach for a Kleenex, but the box was on the floor by the passenger door. And damn it, she couldn't stretch that far, not with her *gosh, honey, you're going to be more than a beach ball by nine months* belly—thanks, Cherry—making itself known. It was too uncomfortable to bend over the console. Grabbing the napkin that came with her coffee, she gave her eyes a few futile wipes.

A fist knocked on her window, and she almost hit the ceiling of the truck. "I know I shouldn't have left, Dad, but—"

She trailed off the second she glanced at the window. Oh. Not her dad, wanting an explanation for her freak-out.

Gray loomed on the other side of the door, golden brows knitted.

She opened the latch, staying in her seat but spinning to face him.

"Where did you come from?" Snappier than he deserved, but jeez, he'd startled her.

"Clearing the front walkway." Leaning a snow shovel against the crew cab door, he stepped close, putting one gloved hand on the top of the open door and one on her cheek. He was dressed for the weather in his uniform pants, a knit hat and a thick jacket emblazoned with the fire service logo. He looked fired up enough to melt the mound of cleared snow at the edge of the parking lot.

"What's wrong? I saw you crying. What do you need?"

"To calm down." *And to make sure no one sees you touching my face like you're about to kiss away my problems.* Taking his hand with one of hers, she peeled it off her cheek. Didn't let go, though. She cupped it between both her clammy palms, squeezing tight. The leather grip of his glove chilled the stress sweat on her skin.

"What happened?" A growl edged the question.

"Nothing I shouldn't have expected. Overheard my dad being grilled about whether me having twins is good for business."

Gray swore.

She sniffled. "And then I couldn't reach for a tissue, and…" This all sounded ridiculous. "Hormones are a thing."

He gripped her fingers tighter. "Feel whatever you need to feel, Ley. There aren't rules here. And people can piss off with their speculation. The success of your business, and the way you make it happen, is between you and your dad."

"But what if they have a point?" The confidence she'd felt when talking to Bree at the coffee shop dissolved into a new wave of tears. She scrunched her eyes shut. "A more complicated pregnancy, maternity leave, double the childcare—it *might* be a problem for the business."

"It's not what you expected. But it'll be something great."

Two warm palms caressed her cheeks.

She opened her eyes. *Oh.* He'd taken off his gloves.

He could kiss her so easily, if he wanted to. If she wanted him to.

His words played in her mind. *It's not what you expected. But it'll be something great.*

The pleasure he'd given her had been great, all right. Stealing a kiss from those lips sounded like the best distraction in the world.

She leaned in. "My dad could walk out of the store at any minute, but... Kiss me? Once more?"

"Once more, huh?"

"Quick. Please."

"You know I can't resist you when you say please." His low voice hummed along her skin like an electrical current.

His kiss teased, tested. A brush. A press. And then more, his tongue urging her to open.

Not quick. Delicious.

Warmth danced between her thighs, tingling, verging on heat.

She'd been craving his touch since the moment she left his apartment, wanted his hands on more than her cheeks and for his mouth to drift to lower, needier, secret places.

She put a hand to his chest, tearing her lips away. "I swear, I wasn't going to do this. It's not fair to say one thing and do another."

He stepped back, taking hold of the top of the door once more. "You said one more kiss. Nothing misleading about that. I know how you feel about me. Or don't, rather."

"Which makes one of us," she said under her breath.

He froze.

Her hand flew to her mouth. "That was supposed to stay inside my head."

"But it didn't."

She smiled weakly.

"Tell you what—you put some thought into figuring out what you're feeling. And in the meantime, when you need a distraction from your troubles, I'm here for you."

She made a face, wiping the remnants of her crying jag from her cheeks. "I'm not used to feeling anything but confident about my work. Zero out of ten, would not recommend."

He chuckled. "But the lodge looks fantastic."

"It's three weeks behind schedule. Normally not the end of the world, but…" She waved a helpless hand at her stomach.

"You aren't responsible for lumber and drywall delays. You'll get caught up."

God, he was good for the ego.

He sneaked another quick kiss. "I know you're behind, but make sure you're taking time for you, too. It'll be easier to be brilliant on the job *and* gestate like a champion if you're doing something for yourself now and again."

"But…"

Grabbing his shovel, he backed away, a mischievous twist to his lips. "Especially if it involves seeing you in the middle of my workday."

She looked up and saw her dad stepping out of the hardware store, eyebrows raised as he watched Gray walk away from her truck. Still tall and lanky from his active job, Joe Brooks made his way across the lot, toward her instead of his own truck.

As always, she saw Abuela in his dark eyes and hair, tawny skin and the set of his jaw. Otherwise, he was a replica of his own father.

Regret flared in her stomach that her kids would never be treated to a "horsey" ride on the knee of the inimitable Joe Brooks Senior. Knowing her family, though, there'd be no end of embellished tales about their much loved late patriarch, the ultimate in cattle whisperers. Abuela moving to Montana looking for nursing work and falling in love with her handsome cowboy was classic Brooks lore. The Flores side came with its own history, too, her mamá's cherished memories of growing up in the San Diego sunshine. Hell, some of the stories even involved the Hallorans—banding together during snowstorms and for barn raisings—given the two families had been neighbors for generations.

Aleja's children would know every word of every memory by heart by the time they were teenagers, just like she had herself.

She forced a smile at her dad, blinking away the last remnants of tears.

"You okay, mi abeja? You left the store pretty quick, there."

Her eyes started to sting again. He'd always called her his bee, given how similar the Spanish word was to the first part of Alejandra. What nicknames would she call her own kids?

A question for another day. She held up her cell. "I needed to take a call."

His mouth flattened. He dug in his jacket pocket and handed her a clean handkerchief, one of the ones he never used but her abuela insisted he carry. "I set Fred and Vern straight."

"Ah." She touched the starch-scented cotton to her eyes then balled it in her fist. "Sorry you had to do that. I should have defended myself."

"Stop. The fault is on them, not you."

But you look so unhappy. Because he'd had to defend her, or because he shared Fred and Vern's concerns?

The scrape of shovel against concrete filled the air. Her dad's gaze flicked past her truck toward the fire station. "Good kid, that Graydon."

"He's been pitching in around the lodge," she said. "With manual labor for me, too."

Plus, his off-the-clock help...

"I heard."

Oof, hopefully not about *that*. "What did you hear?"

"Doesn't matter. What I *think* is how I'm lucky to have you as a daughter and a business partner, and I cannot wait to meet my grandchildren." He patted her shoulder. "I raised you to be smart, and you are.

About work *and* life. Even about young firefighters who look at you like you hung the moon."

She waved off his comment. "Nah. He's just friendly."

"Liar. Saw you smiling at him, too."

She crossed her arms over the top of her belly. "When was the last time you got your eyes checked, Dad?"

"My eyesight's just fine."

Damn it. If he had noticed something, chances were all of Sutter Creek was wondering if something was going on between her and Gray.

She didn't want them to know any of it.

Not until she figured out how she felt about it herself.

Chapter Eleven

"Do you think they know?" Aleja asked, taking a soda and lime from Gray. She would have whispered it, but it was too loud in the Loose Moose. The bar was a Sutter Creek institution of cheap beer, black walls and neon signs, and conveniently, karaoke on the third Saturday of the month, coinciding this year with Nora's birthday. They'd amassed quite the group for the occasion, so had claimed the longest table.

Gray took a seat across from her, colored lights from the sunken-dance-floor-turned-stage catching the irresistible angles of his face. A few seats away, Emma's fiancé, Luke, sat with a few of their other friends and his cousin Brody. The other Emerson was in town from Seattle for the weekend, helping Gray's sister Bea plan her wedding to a Seattle-based financier. Why Brody was helping with wedding plans instead of Bea's fiancé, Aleja didn't know, nor did she have time to poke around for answers. She had enough to worry about with her own life.

Talk about people poking around for answers— Aleja was surprised someone hadn't sent out a community bulletin, based on the number of people curious about her life choices.

"Does who know what about what?" Gray asked.

"Us kissing in public. Twice."

"Oh, did we?" His gaze twinkled, shifting from extra blue to almost purple under the colored lights of the bar. "It's been so long, I forgot."

She nudged him with her elbow. "You're the one who's been avoiding me for two freaking weeks."

"It wasn't avoidance, Ley. Just caution." He took a pull from his beer bottle. "A bit of self-preservation, until you decided what you wanted." He cocked a brow. "You knew where I was."

"I did. And I was…working." And being a chicken. A needy, desperate chicken. She was aching inside, ready to slake her desire to kiss him, touch him.

"You know, it wasn't *just* in public. I kissed you elsewhere once, too." He smirked. "You seemed to like that."

"Shh!" She couldn't be sure the crowd at the other end of the table was out of earshot, even with the cacophony of Emma, Nora and Bea attacking a Kacey Musgraves song on the karaoke stage.

Straightening, he shifted around the end of the

table and took the seat next to her. His muscles-for-days forearm, bare below his rolled-up sleeve, touched her own forearm through the knit of her sweater dress. Why did that feel so good? More than warmth. Something indescribable.

Undeniable.

Want. You want him. Not just once, either.

She did, dang it. He was sweet and attentive and kissed like he wanted to make her float to the clouds. But was getting involved with him worth the complications? Beyond being the topic of conversation, beyond their family members' potential surprise and confusion, could she find room in her life for a partner when she was so intent on parenting alone?

If they were together, at what point would Gray want to play a role in the babies' lives? If he did, he'd have to be ready for people's questions about why he was raising kids who looked nothing like him. The twins' donor father had Mexican ancestry, like three-quarters of Aleja's family. And sure, Gray had grown up right next door to the Brooks Flores spread and wasn't a stranger to their particular mix of cultures and traditions, but that wasn't the same as living it. He'd need to educate himself on how to raise Latinx children as a white parent—

Or you're getting light-years ahead of yourself.

Yeah, maybe a little.

"Did someone say something to you?" Thankfully, he kept his voice low.

"Not about us."

He winced. "People still giving you grief about the babies?"

She opened her mouth to answer but an interruption in the form of an unusually tipsy Nora catapulted into the seat next to her brother. It had taken an hour to cajole her into dark jeans, clean dress boots and a frilly blouse Aleja usually saved for baby showers and family christenings.

"Easy, killer," Gray said affably, putting an arm around his sister.

"You're looking cozy," Nora said, blue eyes suspicious. "What's going on?"

Aleja's pulse jumped.

"Can I get you another drink?" he asked the birthday girl. "It's my turn."

"I'm going to take a pause," Nora said. "My three beers have given me an overinflated sense of my karaoke capabilities."

"You three murdered that song. It's lying on the floor, dismembered." Gray's tone was all affection. "You look nice in Aleja's blouse, though."

Nora crossed her arms. "How do you know it's hers?"

Excellent question.

"Yup, you definitely need another drink." He rose and headed for the beverage line.

Aleja had always admired the skill of the woodworker who'd crafted the bar top. It was shaped like the shoulder and hip of a guitar and kept the place from looking entirely like a dive. She'd contracted the same artist to build the coffee bar to hug the wall in the otherwise completed basement of the lodge. She could have designed and constructed something herself, but she needed to focus on the main-floor dining room while she could still bend over.

"You're caught in dreamland," Nora pointed out.

"Thinking about the lodge." A truthful answer. Good thing Nora hadn't been here a couple of minutes ago when she'd been musing about Gray's sexy arms.

Her gaze snagged on him in the line, broad-shouldered and cheerful, chatting with a few local ski patrollers.

She looked away before Nora caught her staring.

What would it be like to stand with him, cuddle up with him like Emma and Luke were doing?

"Do you think it would be a bad idea for me to date someone right now?" she mused, trying to sound innocent.

Nora's eyebrows rose. "Bit of an about-face. You've been determined to focus on work."

"I know, but after the babies arrive, who knows the next time I'll be able to have a social life? Maybe I need to be open to having a little fun while I can."

Her friend's slender hand cupped Aleja's growing bump. Nora was the only person outside of her family to whom she had granted belly-rubbing privileges. She wasn't a fan of people getting hands-on without asking, but she did want to share the magic with the people she loved.

The night Gray had tipped her onto his bed and

sent her into oblivion, he hadn't touched her stomach like this.

But if he asked, I'd say yes.

Nora leaned her head against Aleja's shoulder and sighed, hand still nestled over Aleja's newly outie navel. "Your pregnancy is making me realize how much I want to be a mom, too."

Aleja tipped her head to rest it against Nora's. "You'll find someone."

Her friend snorted. "Right. Like the pool of available men in Sutter Creek is that plentiful."

"Emma seems happy. And lots of your cousins found people they love. Maybe we need to look in places we hadn't considered before."

"We?"

"Like I said, this could be my last chance for fun. And if you're wanting to be a mom, and you don't want to go the solo route like me, then yeah. *We.*"

"I don't do great with *new.*"

Aleja snickered. Nora didn't do great without having complete control over something. "Just keep your mind open to possibilities."

Gray slung his big body into the seat across from them again. He handed a martini glass filled with bright blue liquid and an umbrella to his sister and shot Aleja a curious look. "Open to possibilities?"

She lifted a shoulder.

His gaze turned molten.

She volleyed back with a silent, don't-go-getting-ideas-here warning. Maybe she was ready to think about exploring something casual and temporary with Gray. But given those parameters, it was going to need to stay hush-hush, even from their families. *Especially* from their families.

"*Nora* needs to be open to possibilities," Aleja told him.

He frowned. "But you're married to the ranch, Norie."

"She's clearly not," came a grumpy, masculine voice from behind Aleja, "or she'd be answering her phone."

Aleja turned in her chair to face her brother, Rafael. With his shearling coat, cowboy hat, and boots and jeans, he was dressed for wrangling his herd on horseback, not a night on the town.

"Rafa!" She blew him a kiss. "You're a little underdressed. Nice of you to join us for the birthday party, though."

His brows furrowed. "Oh. Right." He tipped his hat to Nora. "Happy birthday."

A begrudging greeting, but decent enough given how often Rafa and Nora butted heads.

"Thanks." Nora snorted. "Why were you trying to call me?"

"No one calls anymore," Aleja teased him. "Not even people teetering on the upper edge of millenial-dom."

He shook his head and glared. "I *did* text. And she ignored that, too. So talk to your friend about etiquette, not me. I need to confirm we're fixing the pump station tomorrow."

"Yeah, yeah. I haven't forgotten." Nora spun in her

own chair and sent Rafael a tilted, tipsy smile. "You can't get me down tonight, Oscar." She lifted her martini and tossed half of it back. "As in *the Grouch*, not the hot actor." Cocking her head, she held up her fingers in Ls and looked at Rafa's face through the makeshift frame. "Or both, if you squint."

"Really." What might have flattered any other guy only hardened the irritation on Rafael's face. "Might want to ease up on the blue Curaçao, or your head's going to be hating you on that dirt road tomorrow."

"I'll be fresh as a daisy and ready to go at—" Nora froze. "Crap." She turned back to Aleja, a hand covering her mouth. "Your appointment tomorrow. I'm your ride."

"Oh, gosh. Don't worry about it." It was nice to have company, but at the end of the day, she wasn't anyone's responsibility. It was all on her. "Do your job. Keep my brother from having an aneurysm over the water supply." The RG Ranch and the Brooks Flores land still had one shared well dating back to the early twentieth century. "I'm all good."

Rafael had the decency to look apologetic. "I didn't know. Maybe Mamá or Bree—"

"Nah. Too late to pull them away from work."

"Usually, it's this guy who's backing out on commitments." Nora hitched a thumb in Gray's direction. "Not me."

Gray's mouth flattened.

And yikes, he wasn't kidding about his siblings riding him over his lack of follow-through. She hadn't noticed it before he'd pointed it out, and she felt bad. He didn't deserve the sidelong jabs.

She shot him a sympathetic smile. "I haven't seen that, Nora. Gray's a hard worker." She finished her seltzer. Standing, she said, "Don't worry about having to change our plans. I'll drive myself. Excuse me for a second."

She headed for the archway to the washrooms, crowned with the Instagram-famous, moth-eaten, one-eyed moose head. After finishing her business—when *didn't* she need to pee these days?—she ambled back down the hall.

She was about to take her life in her hands and pass under Chester's massive rack when she bounced off a warm, solid wall of Gray.

Two strong hands clamped around her upper arms, stopping her before she pitched back on her heels.

"I don't know why I wore these tonight," she said. "I'm liable to end up on the floor."

"I'll always catch you," he said, walking her backward past the bathrooms and into a nook that used to house a payphone. Layers of advertisements and posters for local bands, some of which were hung back when Aleja was in college and Gray was barely in high school, plastered the cramped space.

"I'm not sure there's room in here for a strapping guy, a woman and two growing babies," she joked.

Hands on her hips, he leaned his shoulders against the wall and tugged her forward between his spread legs.

"I hope that's not a dig against this." He slid a

palm up, tentatively cupping her side where her waist rounded.

"No. Not sure how I'm going to feel when I'm too big to see my toes, but for now, I like it." She loved her sweater dress, too—pajama-soft and accentuating every curve. "Could have done without your cousin comparing her singleton lack-of-a-bump to mine earlier tonight, but I'm nothing if not a sideshow, I guess." Cadie hadn't meant anything by it, and them both being eighteen weeks along was a special coincidence.

"You're beautiful." Sincerity sparked in his eyes. "So damn incredible."

Oh. Her heart thudded, urging her to lean closer to him, to press into his gentle, awestruck touch. So this is what it felt like, having a man, someone more than a friend, share the experience of the miracle inside her.

Like she was undertaking something sacred, and he was here to pay tribute.

"You can touch my stomach, Gray. I don't mind."

"I wasn't sure." He cleared his throat, pressed his lips to the sensitive skin by her ear.

She shivered, looping her arms around his neck and leaning in.

His hands stayed put, one holding her hip, the other fixed on the side of her belly. "The number of times I've held back from touching you... You're sexy and strong, but soft, too, and I only got to explore you once, Aleja. *Not* enough."

"Not for me, either."

Color tinged his cheeks. His fingers dug into her bottom. With him leaning at an angle, it pulled her pelvis flush against the hard length behind the fly of his jeans. "I can be more than sweet, Aleja."

"I'm getting that." She darted a glance over her shoulder to the hallway. Could the bathroom-goers see them? It didn't seem like it. Rocking her hips, she savored the feel of him. Heat swirled through her body, urging her closer.

"We're out of sight," he murmured.

"Still. The Loose Moose is even less private than the parking lot of the hardware store."

"Disagree. We're hidden enough for me to explore again. A little, anyway." His hand traveled from her stomach to under one of her breasts. His thumb traced the underside, a path of fire even through her dress and the cotton of her bra.

"Agh, I can't fight it anymore," she moaned.

He stilled, so much power leashed inside twitching muscles. "Oh, yeah?"

"Mmm-hmm. But there are a lot of complications."

"And we should talk about those things if they're bothering you."

"Not in a bar nook that may or may not have seen the conception of hundreds of babies, or out where your sisters are dying to figure out why you were sitting next to me at a table with eight empty chairs."

His half smile was enough to make her whimper. "Somewhere else, then?"

"I can't leave until Nora's ready to go home."

"Tell me what works for you." Dropping his hand from her breast, he settled it on her belly again. His smile was bright enough to power the lights the mountain used for night skiing.

"I don't know *what* will work."

"I'm off tomorrow, I'm caught up on my studying and Emma doesn't need me around the lodge. How about I tag along to Bozeman with you? Forty-three delightful minutes—times two—where you can worry out loud about whatever barriers you see between us, and I can assure you I'm not looking for anything you're not willing to give. Yeah, I like having sort of commitment. I'm also good with going real slow."

"Wait, you want to come to my appointment?" she squeaked.

He shook his head. "Just for the drive. It's not fair to leave Penny at doggy daycare on a non-workday, so I'll have to bring her. And dog or no, it would be awkward for you to have me come in with you. But I'll wait in the parking lot. Take you to lunch after, if you want."

There were a dozen reasons why that was a bad idea.

She wanted this too much to pay attention to any of them. "Be ready at nine."

A vibration on the bedside table woke Gray. His alarm, already? Felt like he'd just gone to bed... Cracking an eye open, he squinted at the ancient digital clock that had come with his room. *5:20? Huh?*

He checked his phone to see if he'd set the alarm correctly. Nora's name and a picture of her falling off a horse lit the screen. What the hell? Why was she calling at the ass crack of dawn? His heart tripped and he swiped to answer.

"Are you okay?"

"No. The pump station job is bigger than I anticipated, and I need help. I know you're off—Emma told me she was letting you sleep in for once."

"Yeah, so much for that."

"Our water supply is more important than a sleep-in."

True. But it wasn't more important than being there for Aleja. "I'm sorry. I have plans this morning."

"Yeah?" Her voice pitched into supersonic territory. "What could possibly matter more than helping keep the ranch afloat?"

"Not something I can get into, but—"

She made a sound between a growl and a screech. "Always with the excuses."

"You know, Nora, your life would be easier if you didn't walk around making assumptions all the time. I'm sorry, I can't help you until the afternoon. I made a commitment, and I can't back out of it."

"I swear, if I find out you were moving a couch or some crap for a firefighter buddy—"

"That's not it."

"Well, whatever it is, it can't be more of a priority than the ranch. You're always complaining we treat you like a kid. Maybe it's because you still act like one, with skewed priorities and no follow-through."

"You're not being—" the line went dead "—fair."

Squeezing his eyes shut, he tried to calm his breathing. His logical side knew Nora was way out of line. The rest of him, though, the side conditioned by that Oopsie moniker and his teenage mistakes, struggled to put it aside.

Struggled with keeping his deepening relationship with Aleja a secret, too. He agreed they could run into complications if people knew they were involved. They needed to be more committed before they announced their dating status to the world.

Would've been nice to be able to tell Nora he was keeping Aleja company this morning, though. She might not have lit into him so hard if she knew his reasons.

With his mind whirring, going back to sleep was impossible. Penny was still snoring in her crate—no point in waking her yet.

He managed to fill the hours with a run and a whackload of worrying before heading into town to meet Aleja at her house. The kiss they shared in her front hall calmed his nerves partway.

Screw it, one kiss wasn't enough. He leaned in again, another taste of mint and Aleja.

Then one more for good measure. His hands drifted to her sides as he lost himself in a leisurely exploration of her mouth and body.

"You're beautiful." *Querida.*

He kept the endearment to himself. She'd probably think it was corny, him pulling out something in Spanish when it wasn't something they ever spoke with each other.

Time spun. He lifted her under her bottom, bringing her closer, the soft and firm curves of her against his chest and abdomen. Gentle fingers tangled in his hair. Strong legs clamped around his hips.

And the heat of her, perfect as she ground into him.

He groaned, dropping the dog's leash, pressing Aleja against the wall and feathering his lips along her neck, inhaling the hint of berries.

She gasped. "We... Oh..." Her hips arched, teasing his hardening length. "I— Damn it, we need to go."

Setting her on the ground, he smiled sheepishly. His body burned, clamoring for him to finish what he'd started. "Wish that wasn't the case."

"Me, too."

A crash sounded from the living room, followed by a yelp.

"The dog," Gray said, and they bolted.

Penny flopped on her butt next to a fallen mug and puddle of tea.

"Hell, I'm sorry."

Aleja bent to retrieve the mug. "It's okay. It didn't break."

"Spilled on your rug, though." He cleaned the mess as best he could, feeling like a negligent dog owner.

"We're cutting it close," she said, checking the time on her phone. "We'd better hurry."

Gray wasn't used to being the passenger instead of the driver. He also wasn't used to holding hands with Aleja for more than a few seconds.

When they'd turned from the side road onto the highway and she'd turned her hand palm-up on the console, a silent request for his fingers, he'd almost fallen out of the truck in shock. But then, no one could see them while they were driving.

Ignoring the pang of doubt he got with each reminder of how she avoided public intimacy, he circled his thumb along her wrist. Not all relationships had to go from zero to sixty in a couple of days, especially not with how much Aleja had to juggle.

He suspected she underestimated his patience.

He'd spent years of his life half in love with her, thinking he'd never get the chance to tell her how he felt.

I still might not.

It wasn't as if they were at the point of him confessing how nothing would make him happier than the prospect of rising early to fix her morning coffee, or to have her socks mixed with his in the laundry. Bigger things, too, the things he already looked forward to but that would be even better with Aleja at his side. Celebrating Noche Buena and Christmas or flipping burgers together at the community cookout the RG Ranch had been holding for nearing on sixty years. That was literal dream-come-true stuff.

Not yet. He'd admitted to wanting more physically, and until she was clear on whether she agreed, he wasn't going to admit to just how emotionally invested he was.

Penny sprawled in his lap, all legs and giant paws, her golden-brown eyes begging him for a belly rub.

He gave in, scrubbing his knuckles on her fuzzy tummy. Aleja's fingers tangled with his left hand. Penny's needle-sharp teeth, front paw and leg stump clasped his right. Freaking owned by a puppy and a woman.

Aleja took her hand away to grip the steering wheel.

He felt no less connected.

"Do you want takeout for lunch, or something nicer?" he asked. "The brew pub patio is heated and dog friendly."

"Something quick," she said. "I'm stressed about missing so many mornings for appointments. Hadn't anticipated needing to go to the doctor this often."

"If I can help, let me know."

"You don't need to worry about me. I got into this on my own—I'll get through it that way, too."

"What if someone came along who wanted to walk alongside you, though? Is there room for that?"

She stared ahead at the straight highway, edged on both sides by a gravel shoulder and pristine wilderness. The river to their right, and forest to the left. Another few minutes and they'd be between fields. It was, and would always be, home.

And he suspected this woman would always be the one he wanted to share it with.

He'd thrown a big question at her, so he didn't panic when she fell into thought. He scratched his dog's stomach and waited.

By the time she finally said, "Well..." his pulse was racing.

He forced a calm tone. "Well?"

"I honestly don't know. I deal with life better alone. Navigating a new emotional attachment when I'm supposed to be forming them with the people whom I'm responsible for raising seems like a recipe for being torn in too many directions."

"I...I gotcha," he said, unable to help the thickness in his voice. He said it in the *I understand* sense, but man, he meant it in all ways. And he couldn't keep his doubts from creeping in. Would she feel differently if he were older, if they didn't have the added layer of their family connections?

Those questions stewed for the rest of the drive.

She pulled into the parking lot beside a two-story office building. Stayed in her seat, no indication she intended to get out.

"Ley?"

She pressed the heels of her hands to her eyes. "Sorry, I'm being silly."

"How so?"

"All my talk about being ready to do this alone, and I wish I had company for this. I'm hoping to find out the sexes, and it's just dawning on me that I'd always envisioned sharing the experience with someone."

And he wanted to keep her company. "I'm sorry

I'm no help. Even if it was safe to leave a dog in a car, I wouldn't want Penny to be out here alone and wreck your seats or something. If I count as a friend."

She shot him a wry smile. "You count, Gray. You're shifting into more than a friend faster than I'm ready for."

You count, Gray. Wasn't that a tangle of joy and yearning.

"Wouldn't you feel strange, joining me?" she said.

"If it would help you feel supported and wouldn't result in someone calling the ASPCA on me, I'd be there."

"Thanks." She smiled. "I'll be okay."

"You will."

Still, it made his chest ache to sit with Penny in his lap, watching Aleja enter the building alone.

To kill time, he took Penny outside and let her sniff the small patch of lawn in front of the building. She still didn't know how to fetch and loved nothing more than barking at the tennis ball he tossed her way, which never failed to entertain.

"Gray?" came a familiar female voice. "What are you doing here?"

He spun toward his cousin Cadie, who was hand in hand with her husband, Zach, a few yards away on the paved sidewalk. Growing up, he'd idolized his cousins as much as his sisters. Had he known Cadie's husband when they were younger, he no doubt would have put Zach Cardenas and his Olympic gold medals on the same pedestal as he had Jack.

Small mercies the now ski-patrol director had only been in Sutter Creek for a couple of years.

"I'm, uh, waiting for a friend," Gray explained. "And Penny needed a break from the car."

"Your mom said you'd adopted a cute dog, but I didn't know *how* cute," Cadie said, crouching down and holding out her hands for Penny. The dog did her three-legged bobble through the grass, eager to be loved on.

Gray held out a hand to shake Zach's. "Good to see you two. Congratulations on the baby."

"Yeah, we're elated."

"So's Mom." Gray's mom had helped Cadie out with her son after his cousin had been widowed. Her second chance with Zach was one of the relationships that kept Gray believing love was worth infinite patience. "She's anticipating more Auntie Georgie duty when the time comes." He grinned. "She's also using it as leverage, trying to get Emma and Luke to speed up their kid schedule. Jack and Paisley, too. She's not picky."

Cadie frowned. Her hands slowed on the puppy's wiggly body.

"Oh, damn. Talk about insensitive of me, given it took you a while for things to work out. I'm sorry," he said.

A corner of her mouth wavered. "It's for sure an emotional topic." She stood and threaded her fingers through Zach's. "I mean, we're ecstatic to be here. But it wasn't easy."

He held himself back from commenting she didn't

look nearly as pregnant as Aleja. Putting his foot in his mouth once was enough for the day.

"Wait," Cadie said. "By 'waiting for a friend,' did you mean Alejandra Brooks Flores?"

Gray froze.

"You *did*. What kind of friend were you implying, there?" she asked.

He pointedly turned toward her husband. "So, things okay on the mountain these days?"

"Yeah, they're—"

Cadie cut Zach off with an elbow to the side. "No way. He's answering my question first."

"I'm waiting out here," Gray said. "Isn't that answer enough?"

"Belleza," Zach said, "I know it's a Dawson pastime to interfere, but maybe this isn't—"

"Do you *want* to be in there with her?" Cadie asked Gray, ignoring her husband.

"I… No one was supposed to know I tagged along today," he explained.

Cadie's blue eyes gleamed. "I won't say anything," she promised. "I might have a bit of experience falling for someone who seems off-limits."

Gray held up a hand. "I'm not—"

"Cousin," she said. "Come on."

He sent the other man a pleading look, but Zach was no help. He lifted one of his Gore-Tex-covered shoulders, smiling pityingly.

Cadie braced her hands on her hips. "We'll take your dog for a half hour, and you can go in with Aleja."

"You would?" Holy hell, he wanted that. Badly. "I'd need to confirm she's good with my company."

"Text her," Cadie said.

Which is how he found himself, after sitting in the waiting room for fifteen minutes, being led down a hallway to Aleja by a blonde white receptionist about his mom's age.

"Here you are, honey," the nurse said. "You have fun seeing your babies."

"Oh, they're not—"

The nurse opened the door.

Mine. He wasn't going to say it out loud, but the word, the need in it, flooded him.

Aleja lay on an exam table, semiprone. Her T-shirt was pulled up and her jeans rolled down to her hips, exposing the smooth, bronze-toned skin of her belly. Her nervous smile warmed his chest.

"Have a seat," said the tech, words overlaid with a French accent. The man's friendly grin alleviated some of Gray's nerves. He looked thirty-ish, with warm brown skin and locs pulled into a ponytail. His name tag read Thierry. "Aleja tells me you're a friend of hers?"

Gray nodded and slipped into the chair by the table.

Aleja flipped her hand over like she'd done in the car. He wasted no time taking her fingers between both his palms. Her hand was a little clammy, and she gripped his offered comfort with enough pressure to make his knuckles go numb.

"Well, friend of Aleja's, wait until you see—" Thierry positioned the wand with a flourish "—this."

With the amount of first aid training he had, Gray was usually matter-of-fact when it came to medical issues. Identify the concern, prepare for transport, get to the hospital. Scans and tests and monitors were same old, same old.

Not this.

The wiggles and shadows on the screen, the beginnings of what would become Aleja's babies—a lump formed in his throat.

"Wow," he croaked.

"I know," she said.

Damn, he was squeezing her hand as hard as she was his. He relaxed his grip and brought her hand to his mouth, kissing the fleshy edge of her thumb. "They're beautiful."

"Do you still want to discover the biological sex?" Thierry asked, sliding the wand past Aleja's navel to show them a different angle.

"Yes. After finding out I'm having two babies, I'm done with surprises."

The tech smiled. "Understanding there can be mistakes, you can expect two girls."

Gray hadn't realized what a blur it would be, seeing someone get this kind of news. Aleja's tears, and Thierry's big smile as he handed her a towel to sop up the gel before leaving the room.

"Surprised?" Gray asked.

"I would have cried no matter what he told me." Aleja clutched the towel and his palm. Hand shaking, she swiped at the goop on her stomach. Her shoulders started shaking, too.

"Hey. It's okay for you to have a moment." He took the towel with his free hand and carefully wiped away the smears she'd missed in her hasty, teary attempts.

Pressing the heels of her hands to her eyes, she took a deep breath. "Most days, I've been rushing around dealing with work and then crashing right when I get home, and I don't get the chance to process what's happening. How *real* this is. I'll be bringing two babies—" a corner of her mouth hitched "—two girls, likely, home from the hospital. Alone."

You don't have to be alone.

He wanted to be a part of those moments, too. Being here, sharing this with her, wasn't awkward like they'd predicted. It felt completely, utterly right.

Catching her gaze, he laid the towel on the bed and held his hand a few inches from her bump. "This okay?"

"Yeah." The agreement came with a shuddered breath. "More than."

"It is 'more than,'" he agreed. There weren't words to express the joy of her sheltering everyday miracles.

"Hey, little ones," he said. "I'm your mom's friend Gray. She's going to have things covered for you, but if you ever need to know Joe Sakic's rookie stats or the flash point of manganese sulfate, I'm your guy."

Aleja's breath caught.

A blur of possibilities, of pigtails flying as he let go of a bicycle seat or tossing a softball at a wobbly bat.

That's parent territory, Halloran. Dad *territory.*

Not hard to go there, though. His palm was memorizing the curve of her belly. Every synapse in his brain was firing, shifting from this closeness being a novelty to it being necessary.

Dad.

Aleja would probably laugh him out the door if she knew the thrill running through him as he rolled the word around.

"This… I… Aleja." He spread his fingers wider.

"You won't be able to feel anything yet," she murmured. "They're still like fluttering butterflies for me. No kicks."

Oh, man, once those kicks were discernible from the outside, he wanted to experience them. He'd do whatever it took to make sure Aleja would be willing to share that gift.

Chapter Twelve

"Do you know how hard it was to wait all day to see you again?"

A swirl of early-April night air blew through the door, nipping Aleja's cheeks. She replied to Gray's question with a cheeky grin and waved him into her front hall.

"All afternoon, Ley."

"Sorry I didn't get home until late." She had worked until seven, making up for her appointment time this morning. She wasn't going to feel guilty about having missed the morning, though. Not about the special magic of feeling closer to her babies.

Closer to Gray.

He shut the door, shrugging out of his coat and toeing off his boots. Demanding hands landed on her hips, driving her back against the wall next to her hall closet. Same as this morning, but with no appointment to rush off to, no responsibilities to attend to until morning.

She shivered at the possibilities.

Shivered again at the chain of open-mouthed kisses he dropped from the corner of her mouth to her earlobe.

"All evening, too," he complained. "Working with Nora and Rafael's crew, not being able to crow about how flipping incredible it was to see two little heartbeats on a screen." He lifted her off the ground and nuzzled her neck.

Mmm, yes. He was here and maybe, just maybe, there could be something real between them.

Any space between them was entirely unacceptable. She hooked her ankles at his back and groaned at the tantalizing pressure that followed. Heat flooded her sex. Dios, people did not lie about getting turned on after the first trimester passed.

"This is okay? Invitation's still good?"

Her heart skipped. He was so damn respectful of her needs, from being a quiet support during the appointment to ordering take-out hand pies from that Aussie place for lunch to sate the sudden craving she'd had. He'd understood when she had to rush back to work and couldn't resume the kiss they'd cut short in the hallway that morning. *Later, when we have time to do it right*, he'd promised.

But now there was nowhere to go, and she was

finally going to get to give him a measure of the ecstasy he'd given her the other day.

"If you leave without letting me make you feel good, you're going to be in trouble, Graydon."

"I've been in trouble with you for longer than you want to know." His voice was rough.

She threaded her fingers into the damp hair at the back of his head and buried her nose in his neck. *Mmm.* Soap and shaving cream, and fabric softener from his collar.

"When we got home after lunch and you drove off, all I wanted to do was drive after you instead of heading to the lodge," she said.

"I hope I didn't distract you from your work."

"Oh, as if you didn't!" Cupping his jaw, she kissed him, savoring the growing normalcy of being in this man's arms. "Leaving me with a wink and a promise. It's a miracle I didn't botch the fireplace grout."

Mischief danced in his eyes. "Now feels like 'later,' don't you think?"

"Now feels like—" she rocked her hips, his hardness so good against the hollow ache, but it could be so much better, so much more "—feels like..."

"Feels right."

"Yeah."

He only needed one hand to hold her. The other, he trailed up her side and under her shirt, dancing work-roughened fingers along her spine. "I love touching you." He swore, his voice gruff and awed. "I can't get enough of you."

"And what do you want to do with me?"

He leaned back a little to meet her gaze. Endless depths, those blue eyes of his. How had she looked into them a million times and not seen this, not felt this? She was more secure and more thrown off balance than she'd ever been in her life.

"What I want to do with you?" His throat bobbed. "That could take a year to answer."

"You have five seconds before I start undoing buttons."

"Love you." The words rushed out in a fervor. "I just want to love you."

Her mouth gaped. "Y-you like to put it all on the table, huh?"

He lifted a shoulder, vulnerability written on his face. But there was determination there, too, serious and hot enough to leave scorch marks on the wall behind her.

"Bedroom's upstairs." She wiggled for him to put her down. "Let me show you—"

"Nah." Hands anchored on her bottom, he strode to the staircase and near-to-jogged to the second floor.

She laughed and clung to his neck. "Benefits of being with a guy who hauls people out of burning buildings, I guess."

"You don't know how long I've dreamed of carrying you around like this." He nudged her door open with his foot and scanned the room. His gaze flicked between the stack of Spanish-language romances she'd borrowed from her abuela on her bedside table, the vase of flowers she kept full year-round—purple tulips this week—and the safety vest hanging by a strap from the big mirror perched on her dresser.

His attention went back to the flowers for a second, and then to the bed.

He lowered her to her feet, kissing her thoroughly. A palm grazed her cheek, roughened but tender.

Hooking her fingers in his belt loops, she tugged until his erection bumped her belly. "You're the only person I've been with while pregnant," she confessed, feeling her cheeks go warm.

"Do we need to do something differently?"

"No. As long as I'm comfortable, all is well."

"Good." He paled a little, jingling a single warning bell.

"Sure you're okay with it?"

He rested a hand on the side of her stomach. "I have no problem with having sex with you while you're pregnant. But in the realm of I-haven't-had-sex things… Uh…" He gave her a gentle kiss. "I can count on one hand the number of times I've gone past oral. Literally."

"Shut the front door." How had a hot-as-anything man like Gray Halloran not gotten his fair share in college and the years since? "A handful? Like, five?"

"Yeah." His expression clouded. "Is that a problem?"

Cringing at her insensitive response, she covered her mouth with a hand. "Shoot. It's not a problem at all. You're a firefighter, and—" she waved a hand at his overabundance of muscles "—testosterone. Like, all of it. I should never have assumed. I'm sorry."

"I don't know what to tell you," he admitted. He took one of her hands and dragged a thumb along the inside of her wrist. "But I want you."

"You don't need to tell me anything." One button was open at the top of his shirt. She plucked the next one open, and one more. No undershirt, so it was easy to press her lips against the dusting of golden hair she'd exposed. She lifted a corner of her mouth. "Though I did notice that you sure knew what you were doing with your tongue."

"Long story, but I had a bunch of practice there. Other things? Not so much." He flicked on the bedside lamp and killed the overhead switch. "But I'm game, Ley."

"I'm glad." She undid the rest of his buttons, exposing miles of chest. "Tell me that long story later?"

"Sure. Later." Greedy fingers tugged her long sweater over her head.

His gaze drifted down her body, devouring her in a fevered sweep. His full lips parted, and his thumbs hooked into the wide waistband of her leggings. "Gonna need to remind myself to go slow."

"Or not." Tugging him by the belt loops, she guided him the last couple of feet toward the bed. She lay back on the double layer of pillows and pulled him close.

Light caught on his wide shoulders, shadowing the hollows and highlighting the corded strength.

"You're a work of art, Gray Halloran." She tasted the notch of his throat with her tongue, fumbling with his belt buckle and fly. She flipped her palm, delving between stiff denim and warm cotton, cupping his steel-hard flesh through his boxers. "Want me to kiss you? Here, I mean."

"Next time." He shot her a ruinous smile, making quick work of his jeans before peeling off her leggings.

Hunger, possessive and male, darkened his face.

Tingles rushed across her skin. She kissed him, tangling with his tongue, melting from the gentle caresses of his hands on the bare skin of her back. The weight of his shaft rested on her leg, straining his jeans. Tilted half on her side, she locked her knee around his hip, bringing her core against his hot length, earning a commanding tilt of his hips.

A deep, growling happiness rumbled through him.

She circled against him, moaning her own enjoyment. He might not have done this much, but he was built to follow through on the hot promises written on his face.

"I've been thinking about you, you know. At night." She was like a cherry bomb with a short fuse these days. A mere touch could take her from spark to explosion.

His hand slid between their bodies, under the edge of the fancy underwear she'd sprung for, telling herself she deserved to feel pretty even if she'd be the only one to see them.

You wanted to show him.

Mmm, truth. She had. She *did*. She spread her legs, making room for his wide palm between her thighs. The heel of his hand pressed her mound, kindling the sensitive nerves hidden below. A fingertip traced her sex. Another buried an inch or two into her wetness.

It was all she could do to cling to him and enjoy the ride. Winding her up toward the precipice, yearning to tip over the edge, the plummet through space and time.

"Wait," she said, overwhelmed by the tumult of hands and lips and driving lust. She reached for her nightstand, dug around under yet more novels, pens, notepads. Her cheeks heated at the mess. "Good grief."

He chuckled and reached into the drawer. "I think I see what you're looking for." A condom was sandwiched between his pointer and middle finger. "This?"

"Yeah." She pushed his boxers down with shaking hands. Cupping him, stroking him, she earned a groan in seconds. So damn vital, humming with barely leashed sensuality. She wanted to see him wild.

Braced on an arm, he bowed his head. "That's too good, Aleja. I want to be able to last, make it brilliant. Want you to keep coming back." His eyes glinted. "Or just keep coming."

One rough finger hooked her panties, tugged them off.

It stole her breath, her words.

His lips did, too, traveling a wet path between her breasts.

She dug her free fingers into the V of muscle

where abs met hip. His mouth on her skin made it hard to focus on anything except the direction he was headed.

He sheathed himself. "Bra on? Still don't want me to touch your nipples?"

Cupping her breasts, she dragged her thumbs over the swollen buds, testing their sensitivity. The friction shimmered, a silvered path arrowing between her legs. "All clear, there."

Could a growl be reverent? Gray's sure was. Mouth gentle, he feasted on one silk-covered nipple, then the other. He loomed over her, cradling her breasts in his hands, fumbling with the front clasp. The sides fell open, baring her to him. It felt like... like she'd been waiting to be possessed by his touch, owned with his tender care. His lips were soft but insistent, coaxing her nipples into peaks.

She shifted on her pillows and opened her thighs. His eyes gleamed and he shifted down the bed, running his tongue along his upper lip.

"Te quiero demasiado." It was easier to confess in Spanish how she wanted him too much. He wouldn't understand her. Wouldn't know how close she was to tipping from want to love.

He must have caught something in her tone, though, because his eyebrow cocked. "This the most comfortable for you?"

"For tonight, yeah." Soon, she'd need to think about getting more creative, but now, for their first time, she wanted to see his face, his eyes. The bond mattered, being sheltered and covered.

Though something about the way he stared at her in awe, the breath quick in his chest, a hand caressing her hip—she didn't need to worry about mattering to Graydon.

Holding his weight off her with a braced arm, he settled between her legs. His length branded her.

She arched and gripped his biceps, a silent *yes thank you now please this*.

Better than begging.

Though honestly, she was close.

Fine, she was there. "Please, Gray."

His lips landed on her cheek, and he cursed, either a prayer or profanity. Maybe both.

She expected a quick thrust. Heavy on the enthusiasm. Light on the finesse.

He was big and thick, moving with languid patience.

"Why so slow?" she said. "You're not going to break me."

In halfway, he paused and kissed her mouth. Sultry and deliberate like his unhurried thrusts.

"I know." He sank a little deeper, his forearm still planted so he hovered an inch above her breasts and stomach. "But I only get one first time with you." Fingertips rasped along her jaw, then down around one of her straining breasts. "No way am I rushing it."

Her heart melted, tumbled into a place she didn't want to be in yet.

"I can't resist you. Don't want to." She hooked

her heels around his hard thighs and tilted her hips, taking him deep.

Another half thrust, and he was moaning into her shoulder. Not from completion. Just a man intent on savoring each fragment of the moment.

Intent on loving me.

"Aleja." A feral smile touched his lips.

"Mmm, yes."

Gentle fingers threaded through her hair. He planted his other hand and rose, angling deeper.

A shocking wave of need surged.

He kissed her, and she shattered. Clinging to him, she rocked harder, every inch of his need amplifying the electric pleasure.

Ropy muscles tensed and he shouted her name, need-soaked, reverent. His surge drew out her climax until she was nothing more than tingling, sated nerves and a punch-drunk smile.

The arm he was using to hold himself up was shaking. His head nestled in the crook of her neck, soft hair teasing her cheek. He rolled to his back, an idle hand playing with her hair, the grin on his face suggesting he'd discovered something secret about the universe to which she was the key.

His smile was like honey on sopapillas—sweet, familiar, something she craved until the next time she got to feast until she was sated. A part of her very fabric.

I just want to love you, he'd said.

She felt loved. With his hands and lips and big,

steadying body he'd created a tangled, yearning mess of her, then turned her golden, molten. Treasured.

And for tonight, she wasn't going to worry about what that meant.

Gray was having a crow-from-the-rooftops moment. Alejandra Brooks Flores was in his arms, still wearing nothing but a pleasured smile after hours in bed together.

She wants this. Wants me.

A finger made squiggles along his chest. "Gray?"

"Yeah?" He sounded like he was untethered, dazed, because oh, wait, he was.

"You said you wanted to love me." Her own tone was somewhere between contemplative and wary. "Was that in the moment, or..."

Oh, man. How to frame this? They were not ready for a full-on *I love you*. Hell, he wasn't ready to say it. But love as an action—he wanted to do that more than he'd known possible.

"We've known each other for a hell of a long time. Love's undeniably in the mix for me. I wouldn't have pursued you if it wasn't."

"I don't know if I feel the same way," she said. "Not yet."

"Okay."

And it was. He wasn't so naive as to expect her feelings to develop as fast as his.

"I have the babies to consider. I'm not sure I should be opening myself up at a time when I need to make sure there's enough of me for my children."

"Does it have to be an either/or? What if being open to love and a relationship means your ability to love your kids grows?"

She bit her lip and sighed. "Spoken like someone who hasn't had to juggle work and a relationship and plan for being a parent. You can't tell me that prior to a month or so ago you intended to start a family soon."

His heart sank. Yeah, starting a relationship while on the verge of becoming a parent was a big thing. But would she be as hesitant if he were older? Her belief that her two babies-to-be made a relationship a no-go was hard not to take personally.

"I don't see why I can't be open to something unexpected coming into my life. Something wondrous," he said.

He let out a slow breath. He couldn't control what others thought about what he was and wasn't capable of doing. All he could do was show up for the things that mattered.

Right now, that was holding her. Making her feel cherished. Hell, enjoying it himself. His body was still floating in the stratosphere.

"We don't have to make any decisions today." He nuzzled the soft curls behind her ear.

She sighed again. "Feeling vulnerable is not my thing."

"I want to be safe for you."

Pressing her face into his neck, she said, "You are. But you're also nothing I planned for."

"Yeah, I figured that out when you told me you

wanted me too much." *Te quiero demasiado*. He'd
almost fallen off the bed.

She stilled. "You—you understood me?"

Clearing his throat, he pulled her closer to his
side. "Yeah."

"You speak Spanish? How much?"

"I'm nearly fluent," he said.

She blinked in obvious surprise. "How did I not
know that?"

"I don't know. I speak it with your abuela sometimes."

"I never noticed." She sounded embarrassed.

"I wasn't on your radar, Alejandra. It's okay."
Should he admit he'd learned it because of her? Or
would that make it worse? Ah, screw it. "Back in
eighth grade, I was sitting at the kitchen table, trying to pick out my courses for high school. Mom
and I were butting heads over whether I needed to
take a language. Sounded like a lot of work to my
lazy teen brain."

"It is a lot of work," she said. "I have to purpose-
fully practice when I call my aunts and uncles and
cousins, and make sure I read it often, otherwise I
lose vocabulary."

"Those books look way more intriguing than a
textbook," he said. "So yeah, there I am, glaring at
the form, and you walk in with Nora. You were talking to someone on your cell in Spanish. I knew all
of three phrases in the language at the time, and *mi
amor* was one of them. I was so jealous."

She paused for a second. "I was what, twenty-four?"

"Something like that."

"I was in a long-distance relationship then, with a guy I met visiting my family in San Diego."

"Well, I didn't know who you were talking to, but I knew I wanted to be him," he said.

But I won in the long run, language classes or not. They'd just had some spectacular sex, and now she was naked and amazing and sprawled across him.

He could get used to this.

"I take it your mom reigned victorious in the language-class battle?" she said.

"Sure did." He let out a self-deprecating laugh. "It was my minor in college, too. Not because I wanted to impress you by that point, but because I'd figured out being bilingual is a valuable skill."

"You've never spoken it with me, though."

"Initially? I was too shy. Also, I had a girlfriend for most of high school. Would've been disrespectful to flirt with you. After she and I broke up, I lived in mortal fear that someone would notice I still thought you were incredible."

"And now?"

"I hope it's not weird. Just something extra to share."

"You'll be able to speak Spanish with my babies," she mused.

"If you want me to."

She shook her head. Not a no. A let-me-process shake. "And that's not even the long story you said you had for me."

"Oh, geez, yeah." He swallowed. "Learning all my secrets."

A slow smile crept across her face. "I like it."

"Bit of a comedy of errors, my sex life… Dated someone who was waiting for marriage, and then my college girlfriend and I were both super concerned about unintended pregnancy. We stuck to other things." His cheeks heated. "And since then—"

"You don't have to explain," she said softly.

"I'm a commitment kind of guy, I guess."

"Right." She fell silent.

Thoughts kept popping into his head, compliments and small talk and the urge to share silly tidbits. He'd spilled enough, though. So he held her, stroking her back and cupping the curve of her abdomen, enjoying the drift toward sleep. When his eyes started to droop, he finally spoke. "Want me to leave?"

"It would be best." Regret drew out the words.

"I could stay."

She lifted her head and caught his gaze, her own full of apology. "I can't deal with the questions yet, Graydon."

His throat tightened. "Okay."

"But don't let me forget this," she said, tracing her short fingernails across his bare stomach.

He paused. "Forget what? Having sex with you? Impossible."

She chuckled. "No, how good this feels. You and me, being close, for the sake of our own pleasure. If we do this again, don't let me shove that aside."

If. Crap. "I hope it's a *when*, Ley." He lingered over her mouth, tasting her until he earned a thready moan. "And fair warning—I'm going to do what I can to make you feel this way more often."

Gray peeked over the edge of the loft railing. It was after quitting time, and the dining room construction area was quiet—Aleja and her crew were cleared out for the day. It wasn't empty, though. Emma and Bea were sitting at a folding table, sketching and planning for Bea's wedding, which would take place in the finished room come the following Christmas.

He did not need two of his sisters catching Aleja slipping into his room after work like she'd been doing since the first night they slept together three weeks ago.

He shot Aleja a text to let her know she'd be seen if she took the stairs from the dining room to the loft and might even be spotted if she took the other hallway. There were two entrances to the loft, but with where Emma and Bea were sitting, they could see them both. Time to convince them to move somewhere else.

His phone buzzed, and he checked it.

Alejandra: In the basement talking to Darren. I'll be stealthy.

They'd gotten good at sneaking around in the weeks since she invited him over to her place. Not easy to do, living on the same property as his sister, but it was worth the subterfuge. He smiled, hoisted Penny under his arm to protect her feet from any stray nails and jogged down the stairs.

"Hey, troublemakers," he said.

Emma and Bea were focused on the pile of paperwork they were studying. All he got was a half-hearted "Hey, Gray," from Bea.

"Such a warm welcome," he teased, sidling up to the table. "Have a fur niece." He plopped his gangly puppy in Emma's lap. Penny was getting too big to be a lapdog, but she loved it regardless. And as much as Emma had questioned him adopting Penny, she'd also been happy to hang out with her a few times over the past couple of weeks when Gray had pitched in with some manual labor for Aleja.

Emma yelped. "Hey! A little warning, please. I'm wearing cream wool—" Penny settled right in, burrowing under Emma's chin with a sigh. Emma sighed back and hugged the dog. "Trousers," she finished.

"It's weird to have you visiting so often, Buzzy." Bee-themed nicknames drove his sister bananas, so naturally he used them with relish. "You still planning your engagement party?"

"As if Emma doesn't have it overorganized, dingbat," she returned affectionately.

"What's with all the papers?" he said.

"We're applying to have the wedding featured on a reality show," Emma added, eyes bright with excitement.

Gray cocked his head. "Uh, what?"

"*DIY I Do: Times Two*. The StreamFlix show," Bea said.

Wow. Classic Bea, going off on some wild tangent. "Surprised Jason's interested in that."

Bea's lips thinned. "He sees how it could be a great opportunity to promote the lodge as a wedding destination and for me to get attention for Posy. And I have connections with the executive producer from my Cinderella stint."

"I guess." Emma did need to get the word out about the lodge and Bea's florist shop was less than a year old, so getting publicity made sense. Especially with her professional ties from her theme park days. But reality TV? "It's just—"

His sisters glared at him, and he shut his mouth. Bea could do what she wanted.

For him? No, thank you. Affirming a lifelong promise to another person amid the chaos of a television show was the opposite of what he pictured as meaningful. One day, when Aleja finally agreed to be together—forever, with any luck—he'd have to make sure his sisters realized they were keeping their paws off his and Aleja's special day.

Uh, assumptions much?

Cringing at his inner voice, he pretended to be fascinated with the newly completed rock work and not the woman who'd freshened it.

The woman who'd be showing up at his suite any minute. "Sounds in-depth. Is a construction zone the ideal place for you to plan this? Wouldn't your office be better, Em?"

"Nah," she said. "We figured we'd be inspired by Aleja's magic at work. We're planning the ceremony to be outside, and the reception in here, so we showcase as much of the property as we can."

"It does look good."

"Sure does," Emma said. "And the basement's going to be gorgeous for the engagement party on Sunday." Her eyes narrowed, focusing above his head on the loft. "Why is Alejandra sneaking toward your room?"

He spun and looked up. *Uh-oh.* Aleja had her head down and looked to be tiptoeing in her work boots.

Both his sisters were staring at her with dawning understanding.

"Aleja!" he called out. "I'm down here! You still need your socket set?"

She startled, then made her way to the soon-to-be-replaced railing and peered down at them. "Uh, yeah. The, uh, socket set. I'm on my way out, and need to... To return it to my dad."

His sisters' gazes were boring holes into his back, and he glanced over his shoulder, scrambling for an explanation. "I was finishing a job for her this afternoon."

Bea looked pacified.

Emma, not so much. She squinted at him. "You know, when we agreed you'd work at the lodge, I thought you'd be focusing on lodge maintenance, not providing Brooks Contracting with free labor. Unless it's about something *else.*"

Ha, as if he'd respond to that. She'd read through any protest he gave.

He shot Aleja a quick I've-got-this look. His stomach twisted. What *would* it be like not to have to hide? To be able to toss a quick endearment up to the loft, have her smile down at him, not caring if it was obvious they were sleeping with each other?

Plucking his sleeping dog off Emma's lap, he cradled her in his arms. "I should take this one out for a pee before she crashes for the night. And I'd better go get Aleja's socket set so she can get out of here."

He tilted his gaze to Aleja, whose face was a forced mask of calm.

Emma caught his arm. "Be careful, okay?" she whispered. "Babies aren't puppies. You can't spur-of-the-moment adopt one. Or two."

How much had she figured out? "Emma—" Never mind, he didn't want to know. He swallowed his panic. "Give me a little credit, okay?"

Without giving her time to answer, he crossed the demolished dining room and jogged up the stairs. He didn't know how he'd manage to spend time with Aleja tonight, but he'd make it work somehow. Tomorrow he'd be on shift at the station, and the possibility of going two days without holding her was unacceptable.

Other than his twenty-four-hour shifts, they'd been stealing quiet moments in his room or driving into town late at night to make sure she went to sleep satisfied and smiling like he'd made her day.

But her day wasn't enough—he wanted to share

in her life. And even though he could objectively understand her hesitance to take the next step, her not being ready still stung.

He hit the landing. There was the face he wanted to see the minute he walked in the door after a long shift. The body his hands craved to touch, looking curvy and gorgeous in jeans and a long-sleeved T-shirt. She was so visibly pregnant, it was hard not to muse about her babies. Wondering if they'd both be hard workers like their mom, if either of them would inherit the dimple in her left cheek.

Sight unseen, he wanted to know everything about them, because they were part of her.

She waited by his door, shoulder leaning against outdated wallpaper, lip pinched between her teeth. "I sure hope you have a socket set in your room."

He returned her low voice with a whisper. "I have a small toolbox you can carry out." He sighed. No way could she sneak into his room before she headed home for the night. "Want to take Penny for a walk with me?"

"Sure."

Once they were outside and away from prying eyes, Gray managed his first deep breath since he'd spotted his sisters at their table. Penny, leashed and bouncing after her brief nap, led the way to her favorite trail through the woods. She sniffed at the bottoms of bushes, which were green with spring growth.

Watching Penny spin in circles on the trail, it was all too easy to imagine two little kids rolling around on the ground with her, giggling and getting mud all over sweaters hand-knit by Aleja's abuela.

Aleja walked at his side, work boots crunching on the dirt path.

"Are you all right?" she asked.

He stopped his knee-jerk *yeah, of course*. He'd pretended he was fine around his family for so long, not wanting to admit he wasn't and inviting a would-you-grow-up response.

Knee-jerk wouldn't fly with Aleja. Yes, each time he opened up and she didn't meet him with an equal step forward, he risked getting in too deep. But showing her she could count on him to love her like she deserved meant taking those steps.

He paused to let Penny squat by a tree and snagged Aleja's hand. "I don't know if I'm okay."

Her gaze dimmed. "How so?"

"It sucks having to hide things from my sisters." He brushed his thumb across the back of her hand. "It implies we're doing something wrong. And we aren't." Stepping close enough to feel the warmth of her body against his in the cool night air, he kissed her.

The inch of space she left between their bodies put him on alert. Not station-bell-going-off alert, but enough he didn't let himself get completely lost. "I hope I'm not your dirty secret."

"Of course not." She leaned back, eyebrows knitted. "But don't you think it's easier to figure out without having to juggle everyone's opinions?"

His heart sank. "The cloak-and-dagger operation doesn't feel right when it comes to you."

She bit her lip.

His throat constricted. Damn. This was not the moment to sound croaky and unsure. He swallowed, but the muscles wouldn't loosen. "You know what I do want? To be able to support you properly."

"Gray—" Her voice was as taut as his. "What do you mean?"

"Being able to explain to Emma why I've been helping you with the project. Openly going to appointments with you if you want company. Hell, having you come to Bea's engagement party as my guest, not Nora's." His voice sounded like it was being dragged across a gravel road, but he kept going. "I'm *proud* of this, Ley. Proud to get to be the person you're choosing to spend time with and laugh with. To get to be there for you when you need a hand. Not that I'm asking for a forever commitment or to move in together or anything on that level." *Yet.* "But I've figured out I don't want to sneak. I want to see where this goes—in the open."

Fading daylight gleamed tawny in her brown irises.

"How open?" she asked.

"I love you, Alejandra." The lump in his throat loosened, the words the key to unlocking his nerves. "I want everyone to see it."

Chapter Thirteen

I love you. Aleja's ears buzzed. Maybe she'd mis-heard him. He hadn't voiced a syllable even hinting at *love* since their first night together. Not since saying *I want to love you*. But each time he'd opened his door and swept her into a few private hours of sweet words and sweeter touches, it had been about love.

And now he'd said it, too.

"I wasn't planning on telling you that, yet," he said. Almost a lament.

His cheek was cold under her palm. Something tightened around her ankles. She looked down.

Penny, weaving through their legs and tangling them in the leash.

Gray cursed under his breath and knelt to unwind them from the dog's efforts to topple them over. "Nice timing, pup."

The furry fiend, ever happy to be the center of attention, yipped and nuzzled one of Gray's hands. He scratched her rangy, half-grown body.

Half-grown. Like the twins.

Four months to go.

Two months on the lodge, if she was lucky.

Gray loved her.

And she couldn't see how to fit it all together.

"It doesn't add up," she mumbled.

"That I love you?" He stilled in his crouch, head jerking up.

She covered her mouth with her fingers. "No, all of it."

He rose, looping the leash around his wrist. He rubbed her upper arms. "I'm confused."

"So am I," she whispered. "I want to love you, too, but I'm worried it won't work."

Determination hardened his mouth. "We could start small, only share with your family and mine."

She pictured what it could lead to—to him changing his mind and deciding he wanted nothing to do with having kids.

Unless he sticks.

Dios mío, *that* picture was irresistible. Getting to hold hands with him while grabbing coffee at Peak Beans. Bringing him to dinner at her parents' place. And maybe, after they were together for longer and decided to make more of a commitment, he'd bond with her kids.

"Is it even possible to start small, Graydon? Are you ready to take on the mantle of Dad? That's not *small*."

"I know, querida." He palmed the top of his head, tousling his blond waves. The yearning in his blue eyes nearly knocked her over. He tucked in closer, hand broad and reassuring on her bump. "How can I prove I see that possibility?"

"I—"

The dog planted her front paw on Aleja's knee, looking up as if to say, *Look, he's a good dad to* me.

"I think Emma's already figured out something's going on," he said.

"Which means Nora will find out soon." She swallowed. With her shoulder nudging his chest, it was too easy to rest her head on those strong muscles, to let him take some of her weight. "Okay. If you want to tell your family, we'll see how it goes. Though I'd like to be the one to talk to Nora."

He tightened his arm around her back. "Want to come to Bea's party with me on Sunday?"

Walking into an event hosted by the Hallorans, clearly connected with Graydon?

She waited for the nerves to start.

They didn't. All she knew was she didn't want to let go of him. The thought of attending the celebration and being affectionate like this, cuddled into him, his fingers splayed possessively over her belly, felt natural.

"Sunday it is."

* * *

"I can't believe you convinced me to get a pedicure," Nora grumbled, glaring in Aleja's direction from the neighboring massage chair.

"Oh, hush and enjoy it," Aleja returned. "One day, when you're pregnant with twins and your feet are carrying around an extra twenty-five pounds, you won't see me complaining when *you* offer to pay *me* to get a foot massage and pretty toes."

Figuring she might get more discretion from the staff, she'd even sprung for the fancy one at the Sutter Mountain Resort spa instead of the less expensive salon on Main Street.

Her feet were soaking in a mini Jacuzzi, rotating pressure balls were rolling out the knots in her back and she'd almost managed to craft the right way to reveal her teensy bit of news to Nora.

Guilt flicked over Nora's tanned, freckled face. "Taking an afternoon for myself is hard right now with the ranch's struggling bottom line, and it honestly wouldn't be in the budget if you weren't footing—pun intended—the bill."

Aleja winced. Her own work delays loomed over her head, and Nora's were no less pressing. "The insurance payouts aren't covering what you'd hoped?" The Hallorans were still dealing with the aftermath of a spate of cattle thefts in the area. Her own family's ranch had been affected, too, but not as badly as the RG.

Nora shook her head. "And your brother isn't helping with all his offers to take a chunk of land and some of our cattle off our hands. No way will I give in, but each time he mentions it, I see the temptation on my mom's face."

"He's not trying to cause you problems, Nora." Rafael was curt and grumpy and still struggling with the death of his second wife, but he was well intentioned.

"BS. He knows how much I don't want to sell."

Aleja winced at her brother's persistence. "I've been so caught up with finishing the lodge on time and being pregnant that I missed how stressed *you* are."

Nora picked at a hangnail. The esthetician working on Nora's feet looked like she wanted to tie her hands down to stop the cuticle abuse. "My parents put me in charge, and I'm...I'm failing."

"Oh, Norie." That shed some light on why she'd been so hard on Gray lately. Not an excuse, but it did help Aleja understand.

"I don't want to lose the ranch." Nora pressed the heels of her hands to her eyes. "I *can't.*"

"You won't. You know what you're doing," Aleja assured her. "You know how ranching ebbs and flows." Her heart ached. "I'm sorry I've been so distracted, I—"

Nora's phone rang, earning a glare from the spa employee.

"Sorry, I need to keep it on in case of emergency."

She frowned at the screen. "Not that anything Gray could have going on would be an emergency."

Aleja's stomach flipped, and she poked her friend in the triceps. "He deals with emergencies all the time at work."

Scoffing, Nora tapped her screen to answer. "Yes, Prince Charmless?" She paused. "Hang on, what?"

Another stomach flip. Not the twins-having-a-boxing-match kind, but the Madre-de-Dios-did-my-boyfriend-fall-off-a-two-story-ladder kind. She strained to hear what he was saying.

"Oh, good grief," Nora said. "Are you serious? No, I can't. I'm in town for another hour, and then I have to get back to work."

"What does he want?" Aleja whispered.

Nora covered her cell with a hand. "For me to fetch Penny from doggy daycare. The daycare person needs to go to the hospital for some reason."

Gray must have said something because Nora made another face. "If Mom *wants* me to drop her off at the house, I guess I could—"

Aleja held out a hand. "Let me talk to him."

The two estheticians exchanged a curious look. Aleja sent them a smile and took the phone from her now-confused friend.

"Gray, it's Aleja."

"Well, hello. There's the voice I love hearing." Some sort of fire station racket was going on in the background. "You're with my sister?"

"We're getting pedis. You need someone to pick up Penny now?"

"As soon as possible. My friend is waiting at home with the dogs, but he wants to join his wife at the hospital. Their kid broke her arm."

Aleja cringed. "Crappy. Text me the address. I'll go get Penny and keep her overnight for you."

"How about I join you in bed in the morning? We can sleep away our Sunday morning."

She pictured Gray, padding into her room, plucking open the buttons on his firefighter blues and climbing under the covers.

Covering *her.*

As if they'd do much sleeping.

Her cheeks heated. "That, uh, works for me. I'll wrap up here and go rescue the furry princess."

"Good thing you gave me that key to lock up on my way out the other day," he said, voice a sexy rumble through the line. "I'll see you in the morning. And I don't plan on letting you out of bed until well into the afternoon."

"Ha, nice thought, but I have to work at the lodge in the morning, make sure the basement space is perfect for the party."

"You're underestimating me. We can work on the final touches together. *After.*"

"After what?" she murmured.

"You're on my sister's phone. It might break if I go into more detail."

Her goodbye was more of a squeak than a word.

She passed the phone back with an apologetic smile.

Nora's mouth gaped.

And there's the end of the charade.

"I'm going to need to cut this short," she explained. "If you want to stay, feel free, Nora. I'll pay at the front on my way out."

There was no getting up, though, not with her friend's fingers digging into her forearm.

"You're *blushing*," Nora said.

She could soften it. Evade, even. But she'd asked to be the one to talk to Nora—she needed to follow through.

The hand digging into her skin squeezed tighter. Thank God Nora had stubby fingernails because otherwise Aleja would be bleeding. "Since when do you blush while talking to Graydon?"

"Since he and I started seeing each other."

One of the estheticians gasped so hard it sucked the air from the room.

Or maybe it was the look of betrayal on Nora's face that stole all the oxygen.

Her blue eyes cut deep, a knife of accusation through all Aleja's weak excuses.

"We'll, uh, give you two a minute," one of the estheticians said as the pair rushed from the private treatment room.

Water sloshed from the footbath as Nora jolted out of her seat and lurched to grab her boots and wallet. Pants rolled up and ankles dripping bubbles on the slate floor, she clutched her belongings in her arms. "When did this start?"

"In January. Around when he adopted Penny."

"That was more than three months ago!"

Three delightful months. *Until now.* Tears pricked her eyes. "I'm sorry."

"What, for hooking up with him?"

"No. For not telling you. I didn't think it would go anywhere, so I didn't want to cause a fuss."

Nora held up a palm, a silent *stop it.* "I get you're nervous about becoming a mom, and maybe you were looking to sow some wild oats one last time or something, but did you have to pick my *baby brother?*"

Aleja had asked herself that same question so many times. How it sounded different coming from Nora's mouth, she didn't know. Or maybe it sounded the same, but the condescension and judgment was easier to spot when it wasn't in her own head.

No matter the source, it was unacceptable.

"I didn't want to rock the boat with something casual. But then it became…not casual."

"In other words…"

"I'm falling in love with him."

The truth came out with a clunk, a rattle, the jarring *thunk* of something she'd held to her chest for too long.

"With Graydon."

"Yes. He's pretty lovable," she said, feeling the corners of her mouth play up.

"He's barely out of college."

"Not true. He shows up for work in a high-pressure job. He does what he can for you and Emma. He makes me feel…cherished. What more do you want from him?" She grabbed a towel and went to dry her feet, but between her bump and the angle of the chair, she couldn't reach. "Oh, for crying out loud."

Mouth flattened, Nora put down her things, snatched the towel and sat on the esthetician's stool, motioning for one of Aleja's feet.

"You don't have to do that."

"I want to."

The claim slapped at Aleja like a cold wind. She lifted a foot and Nora toweled it off, then the other.

"You don't need to defend my brother to me," Nora continued, offering Aleja a hand out of the chair. "I know his strengths, and I know his flaws. I know he hardly knows himself, let alone how to be a parent. And him dating a single mom who was his childhood crush is a mind-bender. But when my best friend has been lying to me for months? We talked about falling in love on my birthday. How could you not mention this then?"

"It was so new and undefined. I didn't want—"

Still barefoot and carrying her boots, Nora turned on a sudsy heel and strode from the room.

Aleja didn't let the tears win until after she collected Penny and had the dog at home. Leaning against the inside of her front door, she slid gracelessly to the floor. The dog took this as a sign to play and pounced on Aleja's bare feet, all uncoordinated and adorable with her tripod gait.

"I'm not sure I deserve to be cheered up," she

told the animal. "Your Auntie Nora is right—I kept things secret too long."

Was she completely unhinged, disrupting a decades-long friendship over a brand-new relationship?

Penny tilted her head and flopped on her bottom. Her ear flipped over like a furry Dorito.

"What, stop complaining and do something to fix the problem?" She sighed. "I should text Gray."

From the floor. She was down here, now. Standing seemed like too much of an effort. She patted what remained of her lap for Penny to snuggle and took her phone out of her purse.

Gray replied right away. She filled him in on Nora's reaction. They went back and forth for a bit, deciding Nora needed time to cool off.

Aleja: We can talk to her before the party tomorrow. If we're still going to it together.

Silence followed.

She sat on the floor, petting the dog's fuzzy tummy and waiting for her phone to buzz.

It didn't.

"Something must have come up at work," she told Penny, who stared back at her with a canine grin. "You're no help."

For the rest of the day, she felt at loose ends. Having to entertain a dog instead of being at the lodge maximizing valuable free hours. Trying to nap. Failing to nap. Her mind whirled about Nora, and about what was keeping Gray from replying.

She kept herself busy enough for the rest of the evening. Penny was cute as anything but wasn't exactly the best sounding board for trying to solve a problem. God, maybe waiting until tomorrow was silly. She should just go find Nora now.

Except you told Gray you'd do it together.

The thought would have brought more comfort had he replied to her text.

She couldn't decide whether to be nervous that something serious was going on or if he'd seen the text and ignored it.

By nine, she was drooping, annoyed for the lost time to work, heartsick over Nora, concerned about Gray and generally irritable.

When the dog yawned while out for a pee at around nine, Aleja took it as a sign. "It's bedtime for both of us."

Falling between the covers, she texted Gray again. Are you okay? You never answered me about the party.

Still nothing.

Trace used to do this. Go silent when I asked him something he didn't want to admit.

Reminding herself Gray wasn't Trace, she made a bed out of towels on the floor by her closet. The dog wanted nothing to do with it. Penny wormed herself over to the side of the bed and whined.

"Oh, no. You're not coming up here. Haven't you

heard of the first rule of parenthood? Start how you wish to go on."

A threndy yowl.

"Penny, go lie down."

A single front paw, braced against the bed, punctuated by those little pleading brown eyes.

"You learned it from him, didn't you? Wearing me down until I let you in."

A tail wag.

Aleja was on her side, facing the edge of the bed, so it wasn't too hard to reach over and give the puppy the boost she needed.

"Just once. And no stealing my belly pillow."

It took all of three seconds for the dog to claim the middle of the bed. She buried her snout under the pillow on the other side of the bed.

"Smells like him, doesn't it?" Aleja toyed with the wiry fur on one ear.

The dog fell asleep right away.

Aleja didn't. Pregnancy dreams had been wacky before but throw in a fight with her best friend and AWOL texts from her boyfriend, and her mind went to all sorts of wild places. Cliff tops. Shark-infested waters. A cliff over shark-infested waters. She was too hot, too stiff, too frazzled... Gah, she was going to have under-eye circles worse than Emperor Palpatine when she rolled into Bea and Jason's celebration.

If Gray were here, a solid comfort on the other side of the bed, she'd be able to relax. He was brilliant at rubbing the knots out of the base of her spine, curving around her and letting her melt into his embrace.

She tossed and turned some more until the scent of him melded into her dreams. A hint of citrus and fabric softener on cotton.

"Go lie down," he whispered, sounding more real than part of her imagination. After the kaleidoscope of chaos that had whirled through her mind all night, at least it was a friendly illusion.

Stealing the extra pillow away from Penny, she covered her face and groaned. "Too early."

"Shh, don't wake up." That same gentle tone.

"This dream's better than falling off a cliff," she said.

The mattress sagged behind her. She tilted, got soaked up by a wall of warm, freshly showered man. Strong arms enveloped her. She'd only bothered with a tank and pajama shorts, and his sweatpants were soft against her legs. A hint of smoke underlay his body wash.

Not a dream.

"You're here," she murmured. "You fought a fire last night."

"Yup. Long one. Didn't get back to the station and finish cleaning up until two in the morning."

One of the many knots in her chest unraveled. "That's why you didn't text me." She realized they were alone on the bed. "Where's Penny?"

"I took her out and put her on the towels. You caved and let her sleep with you? Softie." The teasing nickname tickled her ear. "Did you really think I'd ignore your text?"

Not wanting to admit how far into a doubt spiral she'd spun last night, she shrugged.

"Aleja. I wouldn't." Hurt tinged his tone. His embrace tightened and the arm draped over her drifted down to her waist.

"I was wound up after arguing with Nora," she said. "It colored my reaction. I'm sorry."

"We'll talk Nora off her high horse," he said.

A fluttering behind her navel distracted her from asking how. The babies were finally moving enough to feel them from the outside. Taking his hand, she shifted his palm to where one of the twins was busy doing a cartwheel.

"Nora left me a message and—" his breath caught "—was that a kick?"

"Or an elbow."

"Wow." His fingers chased the fleeting movements.

Her heart swelled. In these moments it was easy to believe he was all in.

Could he be, though? "Have you really thought about what this will mean?"

"In what way?"

"Kids aren't something you can change your mind on," she said, shifting to her back and connecting with his gaze. "You're either in with them, or you're out."

Hurt flickered on his face, followed by a seriousness she felt through to her core. "Romantic relationship or not, if I was in their life, I wouldn't walk away from them."

"And when you're out in public and someone questions you for having a different skin color than the twins? Pulls you aside, challenges you? Maybe challenges *them*?"

He stayed quiet for a long moment. His hand stilled over her navel. "We can't predict what other people will do. But I can try to learn what I need to know to make sure your children are as safe as possible. I'd put the work in, Aleja."

"They need to be the priority," she said, unable to keep the strain from her voice.

"I agree." He kissed her temple. "I also disagree. We need to make this strong, too. Us."

"Us." Such a short word, but an elephant in weight.

"Yeah. *Us.*" His lips landed on the shell of her ear. Sparks shimmered along her skin.

Mmm. For all the seriousness of their conversation, she couldn't ignore that she had pure physical temptation in her bed to start the day. She wiggled her hips a fraction, trying to coax his hand lower.

His hand drifted, pinkie finger perilously close to the waistband of her pajama shorts. His hardening erection was impossible to miss.

"Doesn't feel like you want me to go back to sleep," she said.

He laughed into her hair, which had to be a spectacular mess of curls after all her tossing and turning. "Ignore that. I need a few more hours of shut-eye, too."

"Oh, I don't think so. Not yet. Not after this has been promised."

"Using me for my body," he said in a mock grumpy tone.

"I would never," she teased.

"I'd be disappointed if you didn't." A tug of a ribbon tail, and her waistband loosened. His palm flattened above her mound and delved below the fabric. Wasting no time in parting her folds with a finger, he traced a hot path through her wetness. "I want more, though. Take my heart, too. My love. I trust you with it."

She recognized it for the precious gift it was.

She hadn't wanted to take someone at their word this badly since she'd believed Trace's lies.

Gray wasn't a liar.

He hardly knows himself, let alone how to be a parent.

Nora couldn't be right. He knew how to care for a woman. Beyond the magic fingers teasing her tender skin until it became hard to think. He knew what to say, and how to compromise. He didn't question her ambition, supported all the facets of her life.

"You actually love me, don't you?" she murmured.

His teeth dragged along the back of her neck, sending delicious shivers down her spine. The rush of pleasure melded with the waves of magic he was working between her legs. "Very much."

"I-I'm falling for you, too." The gentle torment, the fulfillment promised in his touch—she never wanted it to end.

"Take your time." He sped up his circling fingers, stealing another hitched breath. "I'm not going anywhere."

In his arms, with every ounce of him focused on driving her wild but making her feel secure, she was ready to believe that promise.

"You, ma'am, know your way around a staircase," Gray said as he descended the newly renovated flight to the loft. Pride swelled at the progress she was making. "I blink, and you've built a masterpiece."

Dressed for the party in leggings and a flowy, belted blouse, Aleja waited for him in the dining room, the midpoint of the multifloor design. Centered around a tree trunk, the lower flight to the basement was a tighter spiral of thick planks opening into a wider, airier curve through the dining hall and up to the loft. Chatter and laughter drifted from below.

"It's still missing the balustrade panels. The branches are delayed." She scrubbed a hand down her face and groaned. "I'm having a hard time celebrating the basement knowing how much I have ahead with the floor and the posts and the walls and the nook and the windows. And, and, and..."

He pressed her against the rustic pillar and sank into a long kiss.

"How can I help?" he asked. "Want me to talk to Emma?"

"I don't need you to be my intermediary."

A lock of hair fell in her face, and he tucked it behind her ear. "Not what I meant. I was thinking that instead of working hours for Emma, I could work them for you. An extra set of hands for you to use."

She smirked. "I already put your hands to use."

"As much as I love a good veer into cheesy innuendo, you're deflecting."

Glossy lips lifted, an admission of guilt. "You're right. Today's been a lot."

He frowned. "You don't want the help?"

"No, I do. If Emma is good with you shifting responsibilities, I'll find something for you to do."

"So why the deflection?" he pressed.

"I'm nervous about the party," she said. "Nora didn't text me back, so I don't know how she's going to react."

"Overbearingly, no doubt." And he needed to make sure that didn't mar the festivities. This afternoon was about Bea and Jason, about Emma getting to host a party in one of her renovated spaces, about Aleja having done incredible work.

Not about Aleja and Gray dating.

But knowing his family, they wouldn't be able to leave it alone, not with Nora upset.

"Nora's not like that with me," she said softly. "And I get why she's mad."

"I guess."

"How do we play this?" she said.

"Honestly, I think." He threaded his fingers through hers. "But subtle, if you want."

She laughed. "Nothing about my life is subtle right now. You're sure you want my chaos?"

"More than anything." Her strawberries-and-cream scent was irresistible. Heat coiled in his belly, and he leaned in close to her ear, soaking her in. The idea of people mistaking him for the baby's father sent a thrill up his spine. Was that wrong? "Let people speculate. That's on them. And in the meantime, I get to be with you."

Luminous brown eyes locked on to him. "You're something else."

"Something good, I hope."

"Unexpected. And beyond good." She cleared her throat. "Let's go join the party."

He motioned for her to lead the way down the spiral stairs.

Lip sandwiched between her teeth, she headed toward the cheerful noise of the party.

Her gaze darted around the room she'd so lovingly renovated, taking in the crowd celebrating Bea's engagement.

Gray peered over her head, looking for his sister. Bea was over by the food table—a long plank with three handcrafted tiered platters made of thick branches and slate tiles. Her fiancé, Jason, was nowhere to be seen.

"Let's start with the bride-to-be," he said, guiding Aleja by the small of her back.

Bea latched on to the touch from halfway across the room, studying them with a gleam in her eye.

"Graydon," she said. "You're here. Can I get you a cheese tart? A Yorkshire pudding bite? A side of lies and familial drama?"

His heart sank. "Bea—"

She waved a hand. "Good grief, stop with the puppy-dog face. I get it." A shadow crossed her face. "You can't sneeze in this family without someone being nosy."

"Unless you're in Seattle," Gray said.

"Exactly *why* I live there."

He tried to picture moving away from Sutter Creek, working in an urban fire hall, driving a ladder truck down busy Seattle streets.

Coming home to a house devoid of Alejandra.

Miserable.

"Not my thing, Bea, but I'm glad you're happy there."

"It's a great place to visit," Aleja added, sneaking one of the Yorkshire bites Bea had mentioned off one of the tiers. She popped it in her mouth. Bliss crossed her face, and suddenly Gray was envious of a canape.

His sister's mouth, on the other hand, was scrunched. "Yeah, Jason and I are happy there."

"Where is your groom?" Aleja asked. "I missed being able to congratulate him in person at Christmas."

Bea's mouth twitched again. "He's out in our cabin. Emma put us up for the weekend, but he couldn't take the whole day off today. His call's gone long."

The disclosure was the death knell for his sister's smile. She full-on frowned.

Gray's back stiffened. Jason was an up-and-comer in the Seattle finance industry. Gray was sure his job was interesting, but whenever the guy opened his mouth, it had the effect of parents talking at kids on a *Peanuts* cartoon—*wah wah wah wah*.

And because of that, Gray didn't really know what he did, and Jason having to work during a party he'd known about for over a month came across as rude.

"That's crappy, Buzzy," he said, trying to annoy her out of her funk.

She scoffed but was distracted at least. Enough that when Brody Emerson came from behind her and put a hand on her shoulder, she jumped an inch off the floor.

Bea was best friends with Luke's cousin, a former Olympic rower who also lived in Seattle. If Gray had to guess, Bea saw more of Brody than Jason in any given week.

"Easy, Trix," he said. "Didn't mean to startle you."

Bea brushed the skirt of her dress and put on another forced smile. "Nah. I could smell your ego coming from a mile away."

Brody ignored the insult. "Aleja Brooks Flores. Looks like you've been getting up to no good with the kid here."

Aleja blushed.

Bea planted an elbow in Brody's stomach.

Brody let out an *oof*. "What?"

"I told you the babies aren't Gray's," Bea said.

"I was talking about them holding hands!" Brody said defensively.

"Seems everyone's talking about that," came a voice from behind Gray and Aleja.

Gray spun, making a show of scanning the room behind Nora, who stood in her usual dark jeans and plain blouse with her hands on her hips. "Where's the third sibling of the apocalypse, ready to rain locusts on my head?"

"It must be exhausting, making your way through life thinking everything is about you." Nora sent Bea a stiff smile. "Sorry. Not polite party chatter."

The back of his neck burned. He clenched his jaw.

Aleja's hand tightened around his. "Nora…"

"If you have something you need to say, why don't we go for a walk?" he suggested. If Nora was hurt, it was important to see if it could be fixed, but also to do the fixing somewhere away from the crowd. She'd always been the bossy older sister, but she was taking it to extremes as of late. Maybe there was a reason for that, not that she'd confide in any of them. Did Aleja know? Would she tell him, if she did? That probably violated best-friend rules…

"Sure, a walk," Nora said, then strode past the mirrored rainfall fountain and through the staff-only barricade blocking people from getting to the construction tent.

Inside the tent, the sun glowed through the clear plastic windows built into the canvas walls. It smelled like sawdust and spring damp. Cool air chilled the annoyance burning his skin.

Aleja let go of Gray's hand and poked her head out of the tied-shut entry flap. He couldn't make out what she said beyond "Hey, Isaiah," but he assumed it was a greeting to the on-duty security person.

He focused on his eldest sister, who stood as stiff as the pile of two-by-fours stacked to the side of a band saw. "We shouldn't be making Bea's party about anything other than Bea."

Nora crossed her arms. "Hard to do when you're insistent on using it as some kind of public statement."

"I didn't do anything except hold hands with my girlfriend," he said.

Frowning, Aleja joined them. "What can I do to fix this?"

"If I knew, I'd tell you," Nora said.

"Helpful," Gray grumbled.

She whirled on him. "Helpful would be you not getting involved in a relationship where someone's going to get hurt, be it my best friend or her kids."

"Why do you think someone will get hurt?" Sorrow laced Aleja's question.

Nora's eyes flashed. "You see this lasting?"

The pause nearly killed Gray, connecting with Aleja's gaze and seeing her silently resist her tendency to wall herself off.

She lifted her chin. "I want it to."

Relief flooded in. "So do I. Very much," he said, more for Aleja than his sister.

"How are you at all ready to be a father?" Nora's voice cracked.

"I'm ready to prove I am," he said.

Nora's eyes widened. "That's what this is? Using Aleja to prove yourself, as if she's a puppy to adopt?"

The accusation hit him so hard he almost doubled over. "How could you think that?"

"Because you just said it!"

"Nora," Aleja said, settling a steady hand on his forearm, "I don't think he meant—"

"You sure? Isn't that what you meant, Gray?"

Two gazes settled on him. Judgment in Nora's blue one, trust and hope in Aleja's brown one.

Deny it. Come on, say no.

Except he couldn't. Adopting Penny to show he was responsible. Working for Emma to make sure he didn't seem like a freeloader. And being with Alejandra... He wanted to believe the pattern he was in of trying to be seen as reliable, as his siblings' equal, had nothing to do with Aleja. But could he be sure?

"Gray. That can't be true," Aleja said, words strained.

"I want to agree with you, Aleja." The world pressed in, as if he was in one of the vises and someone was cranking it tight. He wanted to fall to his knees and feed her all sorts of lies to stop her from running away.

He couldn't do that to her. "If I'm being honest— I don't know."

Chapter Fourteen

"Hang on." Aleja took a step back from Gray. Her butt hit a sawhorse, almost knocking it over. The jolt stung. She was more used to her belly being the hazard, but Gray's words blurred her vision red. She didn't trust any part of her body in the middle of a construction zone right now.

He was still, expression shattered.

She gripped the plank of the sawhorse for balance. "What do you mean, you don't know if you're using me?"

"Well, that. Exactly that."

"You *are* using me?" Her tone pitched like the Tilt-a-Whirl she and Nora used to ride over and over when the fair came to town.

He gave his sister an imploring glance. "Norie, could we…"

"Right. I'll give you two some space." Nora didn't look happy, but she didn't look upset, either. What the hell was up with that? Yeah, Nora had asked some important questions, had unearthed something necessary. She probably thought she was doing it for the right reasons, too. But this was not how best friends treated each other. Couldn't she see how much pain she was causing, bulldozing her way between Gray and Aleja?

Once the door shut behind Nora, Aleja gripped his arm. "How can you be unsure about this? About being in this for the right reasons? What about you saying how much you love me and you're picturing being with me and the twins—"

What about me *loving* you, *too?*

"Those things are a hundred percent true." Sucking in a breath, he closed his eyes. "But I'm not so sure Nora isn't also right."

"What does that mean?"

"I actively try to prove myself." He swallowed. "I hope it hasn't played a role in me wanting to be with you."

"You *hope.* Not good enough, Graydon."

"I agree." Taking one of her hands in both of his, he stroked a thumb along her wrist, mile-long stare rooted on the wood chips under their feet. "God-damn it. I need to figure this out, Ley. Otherwise…"

"Otherwise," she mumbled, eyes stinging.

Tender fingers cupped her cheek. "No. That's the wrong word. *Until.* Until I figure out whether I'm in this for *all* the right reasons, I shouldn't be with you."

Her head spun. How could he? She twisted away

from his touch. "What happened to 'take my heart, my love'? Now you're changing your mind?"

"No." He jammed his hands in the pockets of his dress pants. "I still want to give you those things. But if there's a big-ass wrong reason *why*, then I should walk away."

Fisting a hand, she held it to her mouth. She'd known better. Knew she'd start to let him in, give him parts of herself and he'd change his mind. Her heart was cracking open, and it was entirely her own fault.

At least he'd done her a small favor—he'd decided he didn't want her, not her babies.

"I'm sorry," he said.

She lifted her chin, meeting his miserable gaze with what she hoped was cool indifference. She might be crumbling inside, but he didn't need to see it. "This was a mistake."

He jolted, as if she'd stunned him with a poison dart.

She was going to fall over if she didn't get fresh air. "I need to leave. Apologize to Bea for me."

He pressed his fingers into his eyes. Until now, she'd liked his willingness to be emotional. Right now, as he was feeding her a load of garbage, she didn't have time for it.

"See you around, Gray." Giving him a wide berth, she tried for a confident stride.

As if. She was dangerously close to waddle territory.

She pushed at the flaps to the exterior path. They didn't give, didn't open. She couldn't stop in time and collided with the ties keeping the flaps shut. Stumbling, she managed to grab the cords with both hands at the last second, saving herself from landing on her butt.

Humiliation flooded her veins. She was like a chubby raccoon, dangling from a tree branch.

Unbending her arms, she eased herself the rest of the way to the ground. Cold seeped through her leggings and the long hem of her shirt.

Gray swore and was at her side in a second. "Christ, are you okay?"

"I'm *fine*."

"Are you sure? You didn't twist anything, or jar yourself—"

"What part of *fine* wasn't clear?"

He frowned. "The part where you're crying."

Smearing tears across her cheeks with her palms, she narrowed her eyes. "Byproduct of the near miss."

And of you not wanting me anymore, and me letting you get close enough that your about-face feels like taking a hacksaw to my heart.

He held out his hands. "Let me help you up."

"I don't need your help." Awkwardly rolling to her knees, she then stood. And with as much dignity as she could muster, she ducked under the fastener of death. She took off before the truth spilled out. She didn't *need* his help, but she had wanted it, until the point he proved himself to be as unreliable as she knew love to be.

Gray stood in the tent for long minutes after Aleja took off.

What did I do?

He'd screwed up in numerous ways. Pursuing

Aleja, thinking he could make something work with her, letting her walk away.

This was a mistake.

He was a mistake.

He'd heard that one before.

His chest ached, a physical urge to chase after her and beg her forgiveness.

No. He couldn't risk being with Aleja for the wrong reasons. She deserved to know he was with her for her, not because of what she did for him.

If he was with her in part to prove himself, how would she ever know she was truly wanted, desired, loved? Gray had gone through too much of his life wondering if his family really wanted him. He couldn't inflict that uncertainty and lack of a foundation on the woman he loved, or on her children.

His first step to figuring out his head and heart was to talk to his family. He had some choice words for Nora, who'd been totally out of line. But despite her wrecking-ball approach, she'd seen something he and Aleja hadn't. He needed to ask her about all of that, make sure her reasons for driving a wedge between him and Aleja were genuine.

It was also past time he called her on treating him like he was spoiled and irresponsible. The rest of his sisters, too.

After holding in his feelings for over a decade, the thought of confronting his family was a mind-bender. And he and Aleja had already created enough of a stir at the party. Maybe after, he'd find a moment.

Swallowing the lump in his throat, he went back

inside. He spotted his sisters and his mom conferring with one another around a bistro table. Three heads of long, dark brown hair and one of chin-length platinum blond curls.

Ever satisfied to beat her own drum, Bea always made him smile. Falling for Jason and his corporate sterility was so un-Bea, it had thrown the family for a loop. Hell, he bet she understood where he was coming from, given their parents and siblings had packaged her into a rebel-child box.

Emma waved him over. Concern lined her forehead.

He joined the circle, leaning his arms on the tabletop and putting on a smile he hoped covered how his stomach was trying to climb out of his body.

"Triumvirate of sisters. Mom. How's the party coming? Need me to do anything?"

Four sets of furrowed eyebrows attacked him.

He forced a smile.

"Not party-related." Georgie seemed to designate herself the spokesperson. "Honey, you look wrecked. What's wrong?"

"This isn't the place to talk about it," he said.

Bea put a hand on his forearm. "Please. Go for it. Not to revel in whatever's making you frown, but I'll take anything to avoid people asking me where Jason is and if I'm okay with him missing our engagement party."

Her tone was light, but her eyes were dim.

If opening up about his romantic failures could help her, he'd do it.

He stared at the grain in the wood, drawing a finger along the thin rings. "I've had better afternoons," he said, unable to stop his voice from cracking. "Seems odd to tell you Aleja and I are breaking up before I even got the chance to tell most of you we were together, but there it is."

Tsks circled around the table.

His mom gave him a squeeze. "You've held a candle for her for a long time. Must be hard to have had a chance and have her dump you."

"She didn't. I did."

Bea, Emma and their mom exclaimed their confusion in unison.

Nora was silent.

"You were right, Norie," he said. "I mean, I think your delivery sucked, and you owe Aleja a hell of an apology. I'm also not convinced you weren't looking for a crack in our relationship on purpose, which, if so? That's real low. But find a crack you did. A flaw in *me*. And I don't know if it's fixable."

"What's not fixable?" Bea asked. "The relationship? Or your flaws?"

Both? "I might have gotten involved with Aleja for the wrong reasons," he said. "For the chance to be seen as responsible for once."

"Thought so," Nora grumbled.

Emma pointed a finger at their older sister. "Wait. Nora. Explain. What did you do?"

"All I did was ask a necessary question about whether or not he was ready for the reality of fatherhood. He was the one who went on about proving himself."

"Your father and I were younger than Gray when we had you, dear." Georgie Halloran was nothing if not a straight talker. She was also still fully in love with Rich Halloran, who was across the room with friends but watching his family, unease on his face. Georgie sent him a wink and a blown kiss. Typical Mom, confident she could fix things herself. No question where Nora got it from. And unsurprising that Gray had fallen for a woman with a similar independent streak.

"It's not the same as you and Dad," Nora said.

"How?" Bea said.

Gray stared at his oldest sister, waiting for her answer.

"Something to do with Aleja being your best friend?" Georgie said gently.

Nora twisted her cocktail napkin. "I'm not in charge of them. They can do what they like."

"I'm sorry we didn't talk to you about it," Gray said.

"But none of that means it's okay to interfere, Nora." Emma wrung her hands. "Sure, the older woman–younger man thing is a little uncommon, but falling in love with your childhood crush? It's the sweetest. They might have had a real chance!"

"I wasn't trying to break them up."

"You weren't?" Gray lifted an eyebrow at her, pissed off that she was lying when she'd been so mad about being lied to.

"I wanted you to be careful." She let out a frustrated breath. "You're—you're both *mine*. Aleja for obvious reasons, and you, Gray…"

"What do you mean?" he asked, keeping his tone low. "I'm not *literally* yours."

"Of course not." Nora glanced at their mom and then back at him. "When you came along, I was a teenager. Do you know how much I babysat you while Mom and Dad were busy with work? It felt like you were my baby sometimes. My little buddy around the house and the barn." Tears shone in her eyes, and when Georgie put a hand on her shoulder, she took a deep breath. "I always thought you would have ended up working with me. And I guess I've been angrier about that than I realized. I'm sorry."

Well, that was all new information. He'd never understood why she'd expected him to work at the ranch more than she had Jack and their sisters. "You should have explained that a long time ago, Nora."

"I don't know that I would have been able to. That I'd realized it myself."

"It doesn't explain why you were trying to break them up, either," Bea snapped.

"I *wasn't*. I…" She pressed the heels of her hands against her eyes. "It had the potential of getting so messy, and I love you both and didn't want to feel stuck in the middle. I'm so sorry."

"And now you stuck yourself in the middle and made it messy," Bea pointed out.

Nora skimmed her thumbs along damp eyelids. "I know. I screwed up."

Gray's hands were fisted on the table. Emma was standing between him and Nora. She covered one of his fists with her fingers and rested her head on Nora's shoulder. "I'm sorry, too, Gray. I've questioned you about Aleja *and* given you more grief about responsibility than I should have."

"You all could have trusted us to be adults about our relationship. And the rest of my life, too. I'm tired of being labeled with my teenage mistakes. Hell, as a mistake myself—"

"What?" His mom's question was a whisper, but one that seemed to bring the flurry of activity in the room to a halt.

His scattered thoughts froze, a stillness amid the swirl of doubts.

"Not like me being an accident is a secret, Mom."

"Graydon Halloran." Her throat bobbed. "Do you see yourself as being a potential father to Aleja's twins?"

His temples throbbed, and he pressed his fingers against them, looking for relief. "I do, yeah. I mean, did. Crap, I don't know how to explain it."

"Either way, you can't tell me you were expecting to want to join someone's parenting journey. But by the look on your face, you want to. Which means you can understand the difference between unexpected and a mistake."

"I know. And you've told me that a million times. And I believe you. Rationally. But for whatever reason, sometimes the doubts come back. Especially when my well-intentioned siblings keep reminding me of my age."

"My heart doubled in size when you were born." She squeezed him tight. "And you being my baby hasn't changed, even though you've become a man any woman would be blessed to have in her life."

Part of the knot in his heart loosened. She'd said similar things in the past, but he hadn't been able to see the truth of it. "Thanks, Mom. Not sure the second part is true, though."

"Gray—"

"It's okay." Not exactly, but it wasn't solvable in a family meeting. He had no idea how he *could* solve it, though. "I'll figure it out."

By the next morning, he'd spoken to Nora some more. She recognized she'd been nagging everyone too much, not just Gray, and that she needed to better manage her stress about the RG finances instead of shifting her worries into her personal life.

What he wanted more—clarity on what to do about Aleja—eluded him.

Had he been with her to prove himself? Who knew.

And then there was his promise to Aleja to be her extra set of hands. No matter what was happening between them romantically, he didn't want to let her down with the project. She was putting on a brave face with her pregnancy, but he knew work was wearing on her.

After breakfast and taking Penny for a long walk, he tied his work boots and headed to the dining area.

Aleja was with her small crew, getting organized to replace the flooring. She sized him up. Her blank look ripped out the last of his hope that he'd find a way back to the idyllic moments they'd shared, to her actually loving him.

"What do you need, Gray?"

Not to feel like I made the biggest mistake in my life by letting you go.

Objectively, he knew what he needed to say. That he'd thought about it. He knew he loved her and wanted to love her kids. How he'd struggled to trust his emotions and what he wanted out of life ever since he learned his birth had been an accident. That he was moving through it. And a plea for her to forgive him for hurting her in the process.

But it wouldn't be the truth. He didn't trust himself. And until he could, he couldn't ask her to trust him, either.

Swallowing the overwhelming need to wrap her in his arms and hold her until the world melted away, he said, "Assign me a task. I told you I'd help you."

She rubbed what looked to be an absentminded hand where the bib of her yellowish-brown work overalls covered her bump. "You want to work?"

"Yes."

Her lips firmed into a line.

"I'll stay out of your way. But you need the help, and Emma's fine with me working for you instead of her."

"Okay. I guess you can help Darren with the up-stairs suites."

Not in the same room as her, then. Made sense. He hadn't expected she'd roll out the red carpet.

He still ached for what he couldn't have.

"I'm happy to help there. I can on Wednesday and Thursday, too," he said. "I'm at the firehouse tomor-row and Friday."

She lifted a shoulder and frowned. "Up to you. I'm not going to turn away able hands. Though don't feel like you need to be here for the sake of proving yourself more."

He winced. "I just want to keep the promise I made."

"This was not the promise I needed you to keep."

Turning on a booted heel, she busied herself with stripping out the hideous carpet, leaving him to take direction from Darren.

It became their routine. Any spare weekday Gray had, he took Penny outside for a morning romp be-fore dropping her off to hang out with Luke's grand-father while Gray took on whatever task Aleja asked him to complete.

One afternoon, about three weeks after he'd proved he was the unreliable fool he'd tried so hard not to be, he happened to arrive in the three-quarters-complete dining hall at the same time Emma was there, talking to Aleja.

"The lodge crew will be ready to join the workers at your cottage soon. I'm planning on finishing the rest of the work in here myself over the next couple of weeks," Aleja was saying to his sister. She nodded at him, her usual, completely neutral greeting. "Hey, Gray."

Emma's gaze flicked between the two of them, an uncomfortable amount of *why can't you two get alo-o-o-ong* written on her face.

"Hey, Em," he said. "Alejandra. Uh, good you're both here. I shifted my stuff over to the farthest cabin. I'm sure Darren and I will have no problem completing the work in the suite I've been living in quick. Oh, and I have a few leads on rental apartments in town."

"No rush," his sister said.

"Changed your tune from when I moved in."

Her cheeks reddened. "Yeah, well, I like having you around. And Penny's good company for Hank."

Aleja's mouth twisted.

Right. She didn't share Emma's opinion, then.

"Want me upstairs again, Aleja?"

She held his gaze for a long second, brown eyes deep with indecision.

"Or...not?" he asked.

She shook her head, making her ponytail sway. "As soon as Darren gets here, I'm going to get you both to help me with the railings today."

"If that's where you need me."

"Where I *need* you?" Her voice was shrill, and she shot Emma an embarrassed look. "Graydon, te necesito en mi cama. Mis brazos. Mi *vida*." She blanched. "But you... You don't know how." She whirled on a heel and rushed off.

Gray gaped at her retreating form.

"What did that mean?" Emma asked, eyes lit with fascination and what looked like hope.

"She needs me in her life." He left out *arms* and *bed*. Some things were best kept private from nosy sisters.

"And you deserve to be there." She threw her arms around him for a tight squeeze. "Is that true? You don't know how?"

"Yes? No… Maybe?" Hugging her back, he groaned. He'd have to try harder to get his head on straight.

Chapter Fifteen

Aleja flexed her wrist, trying to work out the dull ache from overwork.

The ache in her back, too, strained by her ever-growing, papaya-sized—according to the internet—babies.

Or the ache in her chest, flaring each time Graydon showed up for work, his eyes brimming with apology.

She didn't *want* his apology. Trace had apologized over and over, too, but it hadn't mended the breach between their families. And clearly, like Nora had claimed, the apologies hadn't been enough to heal Aleja's hurts, either.

She and her best friend were working on letting go of Aleja's dishonesty and Nora's interference, but it was still raw.

And her bruised heart was no closer to finding it easier to be around Gray.

In his hard hat, clear glasses and dusty T-shirt, hauling lumber around, he defined *thirst trap*. So much muscles-straining-cotton action. Hence assigning him to the guest room renos.

Out of sight, out of mind.

She'd needed to focus on building intricate balustrade panels, not on Gray's biceps.

Not how she woke every morning, missing his smile, his kiss, his special knack with her coffee maker. Her little confession this morning had been unacceptable. She had to learn how to live *without* him in her arms and bed and everywhere else that made life worthwhile. Easier to do when *not* in his presence, but Brooks Flores women were nothing if not physically *and* emotionally tough. She rolled her wrist again.

His gaze locked on the motion. "Are you hurt?"

"Just a little stiff."

"Is that why you want Darren and me to do the ladder work?"

She shook her head. "Nope. I'm carrying thirty extra pounds on my front. My back would up and leave my body if I was hefting log posts all day."

"I'm glad you aren't taking chances."

She stared at him. "The only chance I've taken lately was with you."

His face fell. "I'm sorry, I—"

"Stop. I shouldn't have raised it at work. Not now, not earlier. Let's stay on task."

Two more weeks. Two more weeks and the dining area would be the jewel she'd pictured back in January. She'd get to focus on keeping her babies cooking, staying off her feet more and making sure her nagging Braxton Hicks didn't get out of control. It was going to be hard to step into a supervisory role, but she trusted her crew to continue their quality work.

Including Gray. She hadn't expected him to keep showing up but had to admit he was doing a competent job, maximizing Darren's ability to do the more finicky tasks.

Why couldn't he be as committed to keeping his relationship promises as he was his vocational ones? She'd be ending her days tangled in his arms instead of working until she was too tired to yearn for his company.

Instead of just being lonely, she was exhausted, with a repetitive-use injury to boot.

"Okay, team," she said to Darren and Gray. "Emma wants the room to feel like we're in a forest, and I think these rails are going to be the perfect finishing touch. Like looking through the branches of a bare canopy, but without making the railings seem heavy. There's enough weight in the room with the log posts and the half-log stair treads. She also didn't want straight lines everywhere, which meant using natural branches. I've spent too many hours over the last week putting these panels together, so if one of them doesn't work, I may have a heart attack."

"Good thing Gray's a first aid expert," Darren

joked, running his hand along the twisting branches serving as balusters.

"And good thing it was a figure of speech. I promise, my heart can handle a mistake on the job." *Just not being dumped by the man I love, apparently.* "I'll take care of the smaller panels on the staircase. You guys work on replacing the loft posts."

They got to work. By lunchtime, Aleja had a throbbing wrist, but a completed staircase rail. Tears pricked her eyes as she took in the branches she'd so carefully sourced and pieced together.

"Wow." Gray was standing behind her. His rough exclamation sent tingles racing along her skin.

"You like it?" she said, not turning. If she looked at him right now, she'd be too tempted to fall into his arms in celebration.

"I love it. It's delicate enough to be all romantic like Emma will need it to be, but wild enough to match the outside. And strong. Safe."

Romantic and wild. Strong and safe.

She laughed.

"What?" He sounded bewildered.

"Your description of the railing—it's what I thought *we* would be, Gray." *And how I thought of you.*

He swore, the abrupt word laced with self-loathing.

"I don't know how to figure it out, Aleja."

"And I don't know if I could trust you if you did," she said, finally turning but still avoiding his regretful gaze. "Let's put on the rail cap so I can see the finished product."

Halfway through hauling the long, waxed plank

over to the stairs, her wrist tweaked, an electric jolt. She winced. Maybe she should get Darren to do this... No. There was so much of this project she was having to give over to other people. This room would be hers.

"You take the top end," she said to Gray.

Of course, that meant an unavoidable view of his jeans cupping his fine ass as he climbed the stairs. Gritting her teeth, she aligned the heavy plank over the angled posts.

Another bolt of pain ratcheted up her arm.

Instinctively, she let go with her right hand.

The weight of the board dropped, landing on her gloved fingers with a thud.

She yelped and yanked, but her hand was stuck. Dios mío. If labor was anything like the pain ripping through her fingers, she was in trouble.

If there was one thing Gray knew he could do, it was manage an emergency. Calling Darren over to help him lift the board to the ground, getting Aleja sitting in a chair and doing a primary survey to examine her hand.

Tasks he could normally do in his sleep.

Completing them while Aleja hissed in pain and held back tears was something else entirely.

By the time he had her hand splinted and was driving her to the hospital, the lump in his throat weighed the same as one of the posts he and Darren had spent the morning installing.

Between her belly and the sling he'd fashioned

for her arm, it had been tricky to circle her seat belt around her. Her complexion gray, she looked fragile.

Had he ever seen her so vulnerable?

Yeah, when she told me she was falling in love with me.

His heart cracked open a little further.

"You okay?" she asked, voice strained.

"I'm supposed to be asking you that," he said.

"You look angry, though," she said.

"I am—at me. I saw you favoring your wrist today. Should have insisted on taking a look at it."

"And I would have insisted that we keep going with the job." Closing her eyes, she dropped her head against the rest. "And now I've hooped myself."

"One step at a time. Doctor, X-rays, et cetera. No point in speculating," he said, pulling into one of the parking spots in front of Sutter Creek's small hospital.

She fumbled with her seat belt and turned to open her door.

"Let me." He gripped her shoulder. "Please. You're one-handed and shaky. The last thing you need is to fall out of my truck."

A long breath shuddered through her. "Okay. Fine."

He met her on her side of the vehicle and put a hand at her elbow and back to ease her out.

"I wasn't supposed to need to go to the hospital until I gave birth," she said with a moan.

"I know, Ley." A fantasy slammed into him, of

helping her out of the truck on the day she'd welcome her babies.

She leaned on him.

For a fragment of a second, his world slotted into place again.

She sniffled and gave him more of her weight.

Tucking her under his arm on her uninjured side, he ushered her through the doors to the hospital.

A half hour later, she was sitting on a cubicle bed, face pale and injured hand close to her chest. A heartbeat monitor hugged her stomach, ensuring the stress of the injury wasn't impacting the babies.

He didn't feel right sitting and chilling in the available chair, so stood next to the bed, rubbing her back and holding an extra ice pack to her other wrist, the one he should have taken a closer look at *before* it gave out on her.

"You're hovering, Graydon."

"You bet I am," he said. "Do you want me to sit?"

"Y— No." Her voice petered off to a whisper. "What if I need surgery? And do you think the X-ray will hurt the babies?"

"They'll use a shield," he said. "The doctors will know how to keep the twins safe, no matter what. And I'm sure the OB-GYN will come soon."

Swallowing, she shot him a pain-edged look. "Thanks for bringing me here. And for the reassurances. But you can take off now."

"I don't mind staying," he said, trying to sound casual. Leaving would be like having a Band-Aid removed from his entire body.

She pulled her wrist from his grip and dug in the pocket of her hoodie. She unlocked her phone with her fingerprint and handed it to him. "Can you text my abuela for me? I'm sure she won't mind taking over for you."

"I'm okay being here, Aleja."

"One more way to prove yourself?"

"No." That wasn't right. He knew it down to his marrow.

"Then why?"

"Because there's no other option for me *but* being here."

Her breath hitched. "Don't, Gray. Don't pivot like that."

"Sorry. You're right. Not while we're in an emergency room and you have a pancake for a hand."

She let out a pained laugh.

He felt it to his core.

Life was empty without her, the happy moments and the stressful ones. Yeah, it was rewarding to build her a railing or perform first aid or hold her while she cried, but not because it made other people think better of him. It was rewarding because there was nothing better in the world than to make life richer, happier, safer for the person he loved.

Why the hell it had taken her breaking two of her fingers—by his cursory exam, anyway—for his feelings to clarify, he didn't know.

I don't know if I could trust you if you did.

Right. He could believe himself all he wanted, but she sure wasn't going to.

"Me wanting to be here isn't helpful if you don't want the same," he said, typing in a text to Adelita Brooks, explaining her granddaughter was waiting on a hand X-ray and needed company, but not to panic. "As soon as your abuela gets here, I'll take off."

Her eyes shuttered closed. "I think it's best."

She spent the next ten minutes tucked in his embrace, though. And when Mrs. Brooks materialized, Aleja didn't jerk away from him.

Huh. Did he still have a chance? Or was she not thinking straight because of pain and worry?

Adelita fussed over Aleja for a minute, examining both the printout measuring the fetal heartbeats and Gray's splint work with her retired nurse's eye before patting his cheek.

"You're taking good care of my granddaughter. My great-grandbabies, too. Not sure why I'm needed here," she said.

He gave her an awkward smile. "It's time for me to head out, and I didn't want Aleja to be alone."

"What, you're leaving?" Her gaze darkened, and Gray got a flash of Aleja in her seventies. "Why? A man doesn't leave his love when she's in the hospital."

"It's what Aleja wants, Mrs. Brooks, so it's what I'm going to do," he explained.

Even if Mrs. Brooks lowered her opinion of him because of it.

The older woman hmphed.

"Abuela, could you leave it alone?" Aleja asked, voice strained. "No soy su amor."

Mrs. Brooks seemed to ignore her granddaughter's claim he wasn't her love and fixed her gaze on Gray. "People who are hurting say things they don't mean all the time. So, respect her wishes, certainly. I'll make sure she gets good care and gets home and tucked in. But once she's on the mend? Don't let her push you away."

Chapter Sixteen

"Are you tucked in the way you like, Alejita?"

"As best as I can be," Aleja told her grandmother. Tylenol was at least taking the edge off her throbbing fingers and aching wrist, but what she wouldn't do for something stronger. She was wrapped around her body pillow with her splinted fingers resting on top of the plush surface. Though it was only six o'clock, after spending hours in pain at the hospital, all she wanted to do was sleep until tomorrow.

Sleep until she stopped hearing Gray in her head, telling her there was no place for him to be *but* with her.

She groaned into her pillow. A warm hand rested on her elbow, carrying the fragrance of aloe lotion and grandmotherly love.

"I've never hurt myself this badly at work before," she mumbled. And now she wouldn't be able to complete the rest of the dining room. Her jewel, no longer just hers.

"People will still know it's your work, even if you weren't the one to drill in the screws."

"How is it you can read my mind?"

Abuela laughed. "Ay, mijita. You think you're the first family member I've had to listen to complain about work problems? The amount of time I spent refereeing your grandfather and your father when your father wanted to stop working at the ranch? Not to mention the first ten years of your parents' marriage. I was your mom's sounding board as she literally learned the ropes. I hate to say it, but an unfinished railing and floor seem like small potatoes."

Aleja made a face, conceding the point.

"I'm sorry you're stressed this injury will get in the way of you putting your personal touch on the lodge. But I'm especially sorry to be the one pulling up your covers tonight instead of a young, besotted firefighter who looks at you like you hung the moon."

"Hmph. You might have a point about work, but not about Gray. If he... If he can't know he's with me because he loves me, if he thinks there's a possibility he was with me for some sort of maturity contest—he did me a favor."

"Hmph. Don't you think people should have the chance to figure themselves out? That we all deserve a little patience?"

"Yes, but I don't have to keep someone in my life

who was using me and my children to look good."
The pillowcase was damp under her cheek.

Abuela untucked a handkerchief from the sleeve
of her sweater and held it out for Aleja.

"If he were using you to look good," she said, in
full Adelita-Brooks-knows-all mode, "he would have
stayed when I gave him a hard time about leaving the
hospital. Instead, he did what you asked. Unhappily,
mind, but he still left."

Unearthing her less injured arm from the sheets,
Aleja took the white square and dabbed her eyes.
"Being alone is easier than dealing with someone
changing their mind about wanting to be with me.
And I won't be alone, anyway." She laid her broken
fingers on her stomach.

Her grandmother did the same, snugging her palm
close to Aleja's. "You won't. You'll have your own
strength, your babies and always your family. You
can live the life you have. But choosing to live it
with less love? It might be easier. It *won't* be better."

The wisdom felt like tapping a wedge under a
wobbly table, bringing it level. It made sense.

And it required so damn much risk.

"How can I trust him?"

"You'll have to choose to. And know he'll make
a mess of it sometimes, too. You'll break his trust,
he'll break yours, you'll choose to mend it."

"Like it's that simple!"

"It is. And it isn't."

"It feels so much bigger, needing to make these
decisions for me *and* two little ones."

"Or you're telling yourself you're avoiding *them* getting hurt, when what you're really worried about is *you*."

Ouch.

"I'm feeling scared," she whispered. "And I'm running away."

"I know." She kissed Aleja's forehead. "I'll lock up. And I'll come check on you in the morning. Unless you text me to tell me you found a replacement caregiver."

"No one can replace you, Abuela."

With a quick wink, the older woman slipped out the bedroom door.

One of the babies kicked right close to Aleja's braced fingers. "Easy with Mama's hand, kiddo."

Another kick.

"I know, I was expecting her to tell me how Adelita Brooks' granddaughters don't hide from anything, too."

Moving gingerly, she sat, crossing her legs. She put a hand on either side of her navel, trying to feel movement from each baby. "I don't need her to tell me that, do I? I haven't hidden from anything in my life." *So why this?* "It's bigger than anything I've done before."

Bigger than her dreams about work, than what she'd had with Trace, than her generous, incorrigible family. Loving Graydon would be a foundation for the rest of her life. Like floor joists but fashioned from devotion and commitment.

Her grandmother was right. It wouldn't be easy.

But Aleja knew how to build beautiful, lasting things. And if Graydon had figured out where his heart was at, she couldn't think of a stronger and more wonderful partner.

The nudge from the twin on the right was sharper than the last.

It felt like a lifetime since Graydon had shared the sensation with her, spanning so much of her stomach with one of his wide palms.

"We deserve incredible things, don't we, babies?"

She could hear her grandmother's car rumbling in the driveway. Maybe she could catch her in time and hitch a ride to the lodge.

Jogging as fast as she could without bailing on the stairs, she rushed for the front door and burst onto the porch. The flashy red vehicle was reversing down the drive.

"Abuela!" She waved, wincing as her strained wrist throbbed.

The car halted. Her grandmother lowered the window and poked out her head. "Yes?"

"Can you give me a ride to the lodge?"

A dark eyebrow rose. "Depends on what you want to do there."

"I want to get my love back."

"Then hop in."

The great hall was lit up like a hockey rink and hummed with the same hopped-up energy.

"This is real kind of you," Joe Brooks said to Gray, surveying the crowd of people busy installing the rustic hardwood flooring Aleja had intended to complete as her final hands-on task.

Gray rubbed the back of his neck, dusty and sweaty from having spent the afternoon finishing the railings with Darren and Joe. "I didn't know what else to do. And my crew members are always willing to step in for family. My sisters and parents, too." Between the people he was closest to and most of Aleja's siblings, and with Joe here to supervise, they'd have the flooring in place in time to surprise Aleja.

Joe slapped him on the shoulder. "I can appreciate a man who knows what's important."

His cheeks burned. "Not sure I deserve that."

"No?"

In for a penny—and not the canine one who was no doubt sacked out on Emma's grandfather-in-law-to-be's couch, living her best life. "If I were smart, I would have known what I had with your daughter, and known what my feelings were, without breaking up with her."

Christ. What would he do if she didn't take him back?

Joe's snort was either amusement or pity. Maybe both. His smile wrinkled the bronze skin around his dark eyes. "I know this about my daughter—she expects loyalty, not perfection. So figure out how to explain what you did in those terms."

"Thanks," he croaked.

"Now, let's get a floor installed so she doesn't insist on doing it herself with a busted hand and strained wrist."

"Yes, sir."

He lost himself in strenuous, sweaty labor. Not to mention a whole lot of good-natured ribbing from his firehouse buddies about how he'd be on kitchen detail for the next year to make up the favor. Familial teasing, too—ribbing Emma about the fact her work boots still had a shine on them from disuse, laughing as Nora argued with Aleja's brother Rafael over who had more construction experience.

It was easy to lose track of time, in work he enjoyed and surrounded by people he loved.

Yet something was missing.

The most important thing—Aleja, with his heart in her hands.

He ached for that alternative. If she'd forgiven him, he'd have stayed with her at the hospital. They could have arranged for this work party together...

"If those boards aren't lined up straight, Rafa, I will rain curses on your herd."

Yeah, Aleja *would* say that if she were here directing the crew instead of Joe.

Gray chuckled and squared his own board on the precise angle her plans dictated. He didn't mind hearing voices if they sounded like Aleja.

Rafael said something back, but Gray was too far across the room to understand the rancher's low-spoken words. He lifted another board and—

Wait. Rafael *replied.*

Aleja was here?

He jolted to his feet and spun around to face the doorway she'd shaped into a wide, welcoming arch.

The smooth lines of wood framed her, all those gorgeous curves wrapped in a soft sweater and leggings instead of her usual jeans and T-shirt. Splinted hand resting on her belly, she wore her work boots and hard hat.

"Aleja." The nickname felt like an endearment and came out a whisper.

But over all the noise—voices, saws, laughter—she heard him, or maybe she'd just seen him stand.

Either way, her shocked gaze locked on his.

What the hell? she mouthed.

Uh-oh. He put the board down and rushed to her side. "I can explain."

Biting her lip, eyes shimmering, she took in Gray's sisters struggling with a stack of boards to her brother and sister Bree prepping the surface by laying down the vapor barrier to a group of Gray's coworkers efficiently fishtailing planks around the fireplace hearth.

"Everyone's here," she said.

"Yeah." His pulse was in his throat. "They love you, querida. They wanted to help."

"They wouldn't have come if they didn't love you, too, Gray. You matter to every person in this room."

The statement settled into his soul, mending some of the ragged tears he'd been holding together for so long. "Appears you're right."

"In particular, you matter to me."

"Yeah? Even after—"

"Shh," she said, tilting her head to the doorway, an invitation to escape to the hall. "I might love all these people, or love that they love you, but I don't need them to hear about our mistakes."

"Right." Taking off his work gloves and tossing them next to a table saw, he placed a hand at her back and guided her through the archway.

She motioned to the small lounge across from the check-in counter, behind which Emma's night manager was doing her best to look like she wasn't paying attention.

The lounge was empty, and he shut the door behind them. It hadn't been renovated yet and was being used to store massive stacks of furniture and the taxidermy fish and deer heads Emma was no doubt getting rid of, but slowly as not to wound Hank Emerson.

Gray didn't care how many departed deer got to watch him try to win back the woman he loved, as long as he got to do it.

"About the floor," he said. "It was presumptuous, I know, but with you not wanting me at the hospital, I needed to do something. Remove one of your worries. If you weren't ready to forgive me, I could at least make sure you weren't panicking about work."

She cut him off with a kiss and a sweet moan of need.

Taking her in a gentle embrace, he fell into her sweet taste.

A palm landed on his chest. She pulled back with a gasp. "Needed to do that to clear my head."

He chuckled. "Kissing you does the opposite for me. But I'll never say no to it."

"Bodes well for the future," she said, mouth quirking for a second before turning downward. "Gray... I've been hiding from myself. From how I was still hurting over Trace, because goddamn it, it's embarrassing to let a years-old breakup dictate my life. Digging myself out from under it took more effort than I expected."

His throat tightened. He wanted to spill all the things he'd been wrestling with, too, but she didn't sound finished. "So where's your head at now?"

Where's your heart?

Her eyes were luminous. They cut him to the core, daily. "I want you to know I'm aware I'm at fault for some of what happened here. I buried how hurt I was for a long time. Told myself it wasn't a big deal and I didn't have a right to be hurt, given Trace was just being honest. So, when you were just being honest, I went on the defensive."

"Aleja, you didn't—"

"Yeah, I did. I was trying to protect myself, hiding behind bravado and all sorts of walls. It's not unreasonable for you to need time to figure out if you're with me for the right reasons. It means you're being thoughtful about whether or not being with me is right for you, not that you're changing your mind."

"Being with you *and* your girls." He rubbed a slow circle over the spot where one of the twins liked to throw elbows and was rewarded with a tiny nudge. It melted him.

"Of course, my babies. The term 'package deal' doesn't seem big enough when twins are involved."

He kissed her forehead, a laugh bubbling to the surface. "Accurate."

"But before we can consider parenting together, I need to know you want to be with me for *me*. I...I haven't had solid before. Or I thought I did, but it was yanked away. I've been running from any hint of being vulnerable since."

The thought of hurting her again destroyed him. He wanted to be the reliable partner she needed. But if he made a mistake?

The quick sandwich he'd eaten for dinner sank like concrete in his stomach. "I'll...I'll probably mess up a hell of a lot. And you'll get hurt, and I'll get hurt, and we'll fix it as best as we can. Can you trust me to do that?"

Chapter Seventeen

*T*rust. Not a simple thing.

"Trust you to mess up a lot?" Aleja asked. Teasing, really. She knew what he meant. She also knew he hadn't told her for sure what he wanted.

The corners of his mouth tightened. "Trust me to fix it as best as I can."

"I do. Truly."

He tightened his embrace. The stability and strength she intended to rely on for the rest of her life.

He smelled like sawdust and deodorant. The tight knot of heartache she'd been carrying around unfurled as she curled into him. She'd been desperate to earlier. When he'd walked out of the hospital cubicle, it had taken all her willpower not to call him back.

Not willpower. Fear.

It needed to stop. Nothing would prevent her from reaching for the man she saw filling her future.

"I love you," she said. "And the next time I go to the doctor or the hospital, I want you there with me. And for you to stay."

He pressed a tender kiss above her ear. "I love you, too. I hope you understand how much I want to stay."

"I do."

"I mean, not for you to be in the hospital." He chuckled, the laugh of someone still processing the aftermath of an emergency. "If you could go the rest of your life without injuring yourself again, I'd appreciate it. A couple broken fingers and my nerves are still shot."

"You're supposed to be my big, tough first responder."

His smile was soft. "I am. But when it's you, I can't compartmentalize."

"This was my first workplace injury beyond a scratch." She dropped her forehead to his chest. "I can't believe it happened now."

"I hope our work crew takes the load off."

She lifted on her toes to kiss his neck. "Thank you."

"I didn't do it to impress anyone, by the way. It all came from a sincere need to make your life easier. To show my love. I don't know why it took me so long to see that."

"Some things we're told, or ways we're treated, stick with us. Being underestimated. Being told one crucial thing and having it snatched away. They can stick, even if we don't want them to."

"They can." He stole a kiss clearly meant to be brief, but she drew it out, lingering over his firm lips.

She ended the caress when she was good and ready. Hopefully the crew was efficient tonight so she and Gray could have some peace and quiet in his cabin.

In his bed.

"It's easy to pretend those feelings don't matter, long enough that ignoring them leaves a mark." He glanced over his shoulder. His gaze snagged on the hideous floral couch Emma had moved from its place of honor in the alcove off the dining room. A slow grin lit his face. Tugging her hand, he sprawled on the sagging cushions and pulled her with him. She landed sideways in his lap with all the ungainliness a pregnant person could expect.

"I'll squish you!"

"You're perfect," he corrected.

"You know what I want to do?"

"I have a few things I *hope* you want to do," he said devilishly.

She nudged him with her elbow. "I was thinking of walking into the dining room with your arm around me, and then after the work crew is gone, going to your cabin for the night, and not caring if anyone notices. This weekend, when your mom makes Sunday dinner, I want to be there. And the next time Dad and Rafa decide to smoke something,

I want to bring you with me. I want real with you, Gray. Open. No fixed end date."

He held her tighter, an arm behind her back and one hand at her waist, moving it around as if he were searching for a little kick. "How about no end date?"

"Yeah. Though we'll still need to take things slow—life will change a lot when I give birth."

"I know." His hand stilled over a spot where one of the babies was wiggling. "But I can't wait for those changes, Aleja. The little things about being partners that mean the most—sharing chores, helping each other. Dreaming and growing."

"Being a family," she added.

"Yes." His eyes were lit from within, as if he had so much love inside it was spilling out. "I want to build that with you."

"Me, too," she said softly. She tried to straddle him, but the soccer ball-sized lump under her sweater made it officially impossible to be front-to-front.

"The last time we got this close, there wasn't as much between us," he said, his smile dancing in the words. "They must be thriving in there."

"We traded some emotional barriers for some physical ones."

He laughed, then sobered. "The twins will bring us together, Aleja, not drive us apart."

"It's taken me some time to believe that," she explained. "I didn't expect you. But you're more than I ever could have hoped for."

"First time in my life I've been happy to be a surprise."

Three months later

After six months of construction in the lodge, silence felt foreign. Gray stood behind Aleja, hands rubbing her shoulders as she examined the completed dining room with a critical eye. It gleamed in the July sun streaming through the towering front windows. All the renovation detritus had been removed, so they didn't need hard hats and steel-toe boots anymore. Gray wore shorts and a T-shirt and Aleja had on a sundress and flip-flops, having crowed she could finally wear a pair of shoes Gray didn't have to tie for her. Penny sat beside them, gnawing lazily at her leash.

A rush of pride flooded his chest at what Aleja had accomplished. "Look at this place."

Sunlight cast shadows through the intricate staircase and loft railings onto the wood-plank flooring. Beams caught the flecks in the river-rock fireplace, twinkling like tiny diamond chips. Not quite as sparkly as the ring in his pocket, but close.

"It's finished." Aleja's disbelieving tone verged on shaky—she'd been complaining about her back pain being worse than usual.

He frowned.

She ignored him and took another sip from her flute of dealcoholized sparkling wine. "I can't believe we did it."

"You did it, you mean."

"Sure, a lot of it was me. But I didn't do it alone," she said. "I was more than supported."

If he had anything to say about it, she'd feel that way for the rest of her life.

He leaned down to nuzzle her neck. "It's gorgeous. I'm sad to be moving."

With all he'd been doing to help with Emma and Luke's cabin addition since April, Emma had encouraged him to stay on the property. He hadn't rushed to find a place to rent in town, even though April had turned to May, May had become June, and now it was July and he had to admit he was attached to his little cabin.

Much of the attachment was from sharing the space with Aleja, who'd slept over more often than not.

"What time's your appointment to sign the lease tomorrow?" she asked, shifting her weight and hissing out a breath.

"Eleven," he said. He pressed a thumb against a knot above her hip.

Penny glanced at him with a dubious expression, a clear, canine version of: *She's still pretending nothing's amiss?*

She is, Pen, she is.

Aleja had been grimacing a few times an hour. He'd gotten well used to the grumpy expression that crossed her face when she got Braxton Hicks contractions and was forced to go sit down. But this was different. The strain on her face and in her posture was more serious than he'd seen before.

She'd passed thirty-seven weeks a couple days ago, and both babies were blessedly head down, so they didn't need to panic. It wasn't close to the ten-minute mark where they'd need to go to the hospital. Until those grimaces started coming faster, he'd wait until she was ready to tell him she'd been having contractions all day.

His heart rate picked up. *Contractions. Go time.* If he didn't get down on one knee soon, he'd be waiting until after the babies were born.

"What if…" She let out a slow breath. "What if you *didn't* sign the lease?"

"I need a place to live, Ley. Emma needs her cabin back."

"I know, but I've been thinking…" She laced her fingers in his and tugged him toward the circle of suede couches and velvet chairs in front of the stone hearth, easing across the otherwise furniture-less space with the slow mosey she'd adopted since one of the babies had dropped a month ago.

Penny flopped on the plush area rug. He sat sideways on one of the deep couches, leaning against an arm with his leg stretched out along the back. He patted the soft leather in front of him.

She sat in the cradle of his thighs and stretched her legs out, too.

"What have you been thinking about?" He slid his hands under her belly and lifted, taking some of the weight.

"Mmm, magic hands." She leaned her head back against his shoulder and moaned in satisfaction.

"You've been thinking about my magic hands?"

"No, I've been thinking about you renting a place in town."

"Like we talked about. Close to your house so I can help. Going slow. Separate places."

Her stomach tightened against his palms, harder than he'd ever felt it tense.

Her breath hitched.

"Are you sure you don't want to have a lie down in the cabin?" he asked. "Or head home?"

She shook her head and shifted on the couch, whimpering a little. "I want—" she sucked in a breath through her teeth "—to talk about your appointment tomorrow."

Something told him he wasn't going to make it and would be imposing on his sister's generosity for another few weeks while he found a new rental option.

Penny slunk over to them and rested her head on Aleja's leg, eyes imploring.

Aleja gripped Penny's shaggy scruff and let out a slow breath.

Gray checked his watch.

Twelve minutes.

Thankfully, with him sitting behind her, she couldn't see the face he made. He'd overshot his window. No way was he proposing when she was in labor.

He kept one hand in place supporting the swell of the babies and slipped the other between them to rub her back again.

"If I miss my chance to sign the lease, it won't be the end of the world. I'll figure something out."

"You're planning on missing it?"

He snorted. She was still sticking to her nothing-to-see-here story. "Seems like we might be occupied with something else."

"Mmm," she said. "Yeah, on that note…"

He held his breath. Something about her being on the verge of admitting she was having contractions felt meaningful. Almost sacred.

She looked over her shoulder at him, eyebrow raised. "Breathe, Gray. Hee hee, hoo."

"The labor coach said not to breathe that way," he teased.

She spun ninety degrees so that her back was against his leg and her feet were on the ground. Penny glommed onto her again, shimmying between Aleja's knees and using her thigh as a pillow. A Velcro dog, through and through.

"You ready for this?" she murmured, cheeks a little pale.

"I am, if you're ready to call it official."

Her eyes shuttered. "I… So eventually these babies are going to arrive—"

"Eventually?"

She swatted him with a hand. "Yes. Not any time soon. I'm just having Braxton Hicks. *Anyway*, I'm going to have to take them home. The babies, not the Braxton Hicks."

He chuckled. "I assumed."

"And when I take them home, I want you to be there."

"I was hoping that was still the plan."

"And I don't want you to leave."

Joy flooded his heart. "Okay. I'll stay as long as you want me to."

Dark eyes settled on his. "Indefinitely?"

"You mean move in with you?"

"Yes."

"My work boots alongside yours in the front closet?" he said.

"Well, you're sure as hell not leaving them lying around," she teased.

"Trading off night feeds?"

"Mmm, yes please."

"Replacing your coffee maker with mine so I can bring you even better coffee in bed?"

Her gaze turned velvet soft. "Gray…"

"I know. Sounds like heaven." He felt his smile wobble. "Are you sure?"

She frowned. "Are you unsure?"

"Are you kidding? I'll have my stuff in there so fast, you'll think I've lived there for a year. But I wanted to make sure this wasn't a spur-of-the-labor-moment decision."

"What's this 'labor' business you're talking about?"

"Alejandra…" All she'd been talking about for the past two months was getting to full-term and finally giving birth, so her reluctance to admit what was happening was odd.

"Less EMT, more just my boyfriend, please."

"Well, your boyfriend thinks moving into your place—making it ours—would be incredible."

"We should go pack, then," she said. "We can spend the night together tonight, and—" she froze, eyes widening "—oh, dear."

"What's wrong?" Her stomach wasn't as tight

under his hand, so he didn't think she was having another contraction yet.

Her cheeks flared pink. "I might need to get Emma another couch."

"What?"

"My water broke."

A thrill ran through him. He brushed a strand of hair off her forehead. "It's happening. We're going to meet your babies."

"I want to, so much." She sucked in a breath. "And I'm scared."

"You can do this, querida. Anything you need, it's yours," he said, drawing a slow circle on her back.

She clung to his hand. "Just you, Gray. You're enough."

"Then you're set. I've always been yours."

Aleja woke from her nap with a start, levering partway upright before a stab of pain reminded her moving at anything more than a glacial speed was the enemy. She lowered herself back to prone with a hiss.

"Easy, Aleja." Gray's soothing voice drifted from somewhere behind her.

After four days of trying to sleep and recover at the hospital amidst beeping monitors and rolling wheels in the hallway and voices drifting from the nurses' station, the quiet of the house was almost eerie.

She knew the silence—the lack of fussing, to be specific—meant she should keep napping, but she couldn't. Partly because her chest was starting to ache, a sign it was feeding time. Mostly because she craved the sight of her new little family.

Maybe it came with swimming in a vat of postpartum hormones, but no sight was sweeter than Gray cuddling with the babies.

"Gray?" she called out.

He materialized, settling on the edge of the chest she used as a living room coffee table. His rumpled clothes and I-survived-a-typhoon hair were something to behold, but so long as the tiny, swaddled sprouts were peaceful, tucked side by side into the crook of a muscled arm, nothing else mattered.

She reached out a hand, tracing a finger down one impossibly soft cheek, then another.

"Hey, little ones," she said. So small, both around five and a half pounds. Healthy, though, after some initial panic. "Lunchtime?"

"I doubt you'll get any complaints," he said.

"I should sit up, but I'm stuck," she lamented, rising on an elbow. "Still kinda feels like my insides are going to fall out."

"Seems expected, given you got the joy of vaginal and caesarean delivery," he said. "Here, superstar, let me help."

"You have your arms full."

"I've got enough arms for all of you." He knelt on the floor, the twins secure on one side and his other hand wedged under her, taking her weight as she rose so she didn't have to strain her healing stomach.

Aleja was still processing the intensity of the delivery. Things had gone from *both babies are in a good position* to having her firstborn on her chest and preparing to push again to *baby B's vitals are dropping* so fast, she'd barely had time to think.

Gray had been the one constant throughout the blur. All that day, and each day since. He'd taken holidays and asked Emma to dog-sit Penny so they could have a couple of weeks to focus on the twins and Aleja's recovery.

"I love you," she whispered.

"I love you, too." He shifted and went to sit next to her. A box fell out of his pocket and onto the area rug under the chest.

A small, Tiffany-blue box, tied in a white ribbon.

She froze, her physical discomfort melting away in the presence of that blue and that bow and this man wearing the most uncertain expression.

He snatched the box with his free hand. "You weren't supposed to see this yet."

"No? When was I, exactly?" she asked.

Box clutched in his fist, he ran his knuckles over his four days of beard. "When we were celebrating the lodge completion. But you went into labor and were busy delivering Julieta. And the transition to the surgery, and Mireya in the NICU... Then feeding and no sleep and we've both been in sweatpants with bedhead. You deserve a better proposal than this, Aleja."

She snuggled in close. "You have never looked more attractive to me than you do while holding our babies."

"*Our* babies?" he choked out.

"Ours." She laid her left hand on the seam where

the two swaddles met and wiggled her ring finger. "And our life together. I can't wait for it, Gray."

He fumbled to open the box and held out the ring. The solitaire glinted in the recessed lights overhead.

Two sets of eyes blinked open, focusing with newborn intensity on Graydon's face.

"I know, babies. I like to stare at him, too," Aleja said. "What do you think, should your mamá marry your daddy?"

A coo from Julieta, her full head of dark hair covered in a violet cap knitted by Brody Emerson, of all people. He'd made a fuchsia one for Mireya, who let out a squawk, her face turning the same color as the vivid yarn.

"I'm going to take that as a request for lunch, not a criticism of my proposal skills," Gray said.

"I don't know, she has a point. I haven't heard a proposal yet," Aleja teased, wiggling her finger again.

"I'm already the luckiest man in the world," he said. "Will you marry me and make it official?"

"If it means I get to be a family with you and the twins for the rest of my life? A hundred times, yes."

* * * * *

*Don't miss the previous titles in Laurel Greer's
Sutter Creek, Montana miniseries:*

From Exes to Expecting
A Father for Her Child
Holiday by Candlelight
Their Nine-Month Surprise
In Service of Love
Snowbound with the Sheriff
Twelve Dates of Christmas

Available now from Harlequin Special Edition!

#2923 THE OTHER HOLLISTER MAN
Men of the West • by Stella Bagwell

Rancher Jack Hollister travels to Arizona to discover if the family on Three Rivers Ranch might possibly be a long-lost relation. He isn't looking for love—until he sees Vanessa Richardson.

#2924 IN THE RING WITH THE MAVERICK
Montana Mavericks: Brothers & Broncos • by Kathy Douglass

Two rodeo riders—cowboy Jack Burris and rodeo queen Audrey Hawkins—compete for the same prize all the while battling their feelings for each other. Sparks fly as they discover that the best prize is the love that grows between them.

#2925 LESSONS IN FATHERHOOD
Home to Oak Hollow • by Makenna Lee

When Nicholas Weller finds a baby in his art gallery, he's shocked to find out the baby is his. Emma Blake agrees to teach this confirmed bachelor how to be a father, but after the loss of her husband and child, can she learn to love again?

#2926 IT STARTED WITH A PUPPY
Furever Yours • by Christy Jeffries

Shy and unobtrusive Elise Mackenzie is finally living life under her own control, while charming and successful Harris Vega has never met a fixer-upper house he couldn't remodel. Elise is finally coming into her own but does Harris see her as just another project—or is there something more between them?

#2927 BE CAREFUL WHAT YOU WISH FOR
Lucky Stars • by Elizabeth Bevarly

When Chance wished for a million dollars as a teenager, he never expected it to come true—especially not via his late brother's twins, who are now his responsibility. Luckily, Poppy Digby has known the twins all their lives and agrees to stay—just for a few days!—but they each find themselves longing for more time...

#2928 EXPECTING HER EX'S BABY
Sutton's Place • by Shannon Stacey

Lane Thompson and Evie Sutton were married once and that didn't work out. But resisting each other hasn't worked out very well, either, and now they're having a baby. Can they make it work this time around? Or will old wounds once again tear them apart?

HSECNM0622

"He cannot be serious." Tansy stared at the front page of the local *Hill Country Gazette* in horror. At the far too flattering picture of Dane Knudson. And that smile. That smug, "That's right, I'm superhot and I know it" smile that set her teeth on edge. "What is he thinking?"

"He who?" Tansy's sister, Astrid, sat across the kitchen table with Beeswax, their massive orange cat, occupying her lap.

"Dane." Tansy wiggled the newspaper. "Who else?"

"What did he do now?" Aunt Camellia asked.

"This." Tansy shook the newspaper again. "'While continuing to produce their award-winning clover honey,'" she read, "'Viking Honey will be expanding operations and combining their Viking ancestry and Texas heritage—'"

Aunt Camellia joined them at the table. "All the Viking this and Viking that. That boy is pure Texan."

"The Viking thing is a marketing gimmick," Tansy agreed.

"A smart one." Astrid winced at the glare Tansy shot her way. "What about this has you so worked up, Tansy?"

"I hadn't gotten there, yet." Tansy held up one finger as she continued, "'Combining their Viking ancestry and Texas heritage for a one-of-a-kind event venue and riverfront cabins ready for nature-loving guests by next fall.'"

All at once, the room froze. *Finally.* She watched as, one by one, they realized why this was a bad thing.

Two years of scorching heat and drought had left Honey Hill Farms' apiaries in a precarious position. Not just the bees—the family farm itself.

"It's almost as if he doesn't understand or…or care about the bees." Astrid looked sincerely crestfallen.

"He *doesn't* care about the bees." Tansy nodded. "If he did, this wouldn't be happening." She scanned the paper again—but not the photo. His smile only added insult to injury.

To Dane, life was a game and toying with people's emotions was all part of it. Over and over again, she'd invested time and energy and hours of hard work, and he'd just sort of winged it. *Always.* As far as Tansy knew, he'd never suffered any consequences for his lackluster efforts. No, the great Dane Knudson could charm his way through pretty much any situation. But what would he know about hard work or facing consequences when his family made a good portion of their income off a stolen Hill Honey recipe?

Don't miss
The Sweetest Thing *by Sasha Summers,*
available June 2022 wherever
HQN books and ebooks are sold.

Harlequin.com

"Wait, what?" he interrupted again. "Logan worked for a
tech firm?"

Although his brother had taught himself to code when he
was still in middle school, and he'd been a good hacker of
the dirty tricks variety when they were teenagers, Chance
couldn't see him ever living the cubicle lifestyle for a steady
paycheck.

"Yes," Poppy said. "And he developed a computer program
several years ago that allowed companies to legally plunder
and sell all kinds of personal information and online habits of
anyone who used their websites. It goes without saying that it
was worth a gold mine to corporate America. And corporate
America paid your brother a gold mine for it."

Okay, that did actually sound like something Logan would
have been able to do. Chance probably shouldn't be surprised
that his brother would turn his gift for hacking into making a
pile of money.

Poppy pulled another piece of paper from the collection in front of her. "I have another statement that's been prepared for your trust, Mr. Foley."

He started to correct Poppy's "Mr. Foley" again, but the other part of her statement sank in too quickly. "What do you mean my trust?"

"I mean your brother and sister-in-law have put funds into a trust for you, as well."

He didn't know what to say. So he said nothing, only gazed back at Poppy, confused as hell.

When he said nothing, she continued. "The children's trust will begin to gradually revert to them when they reach the age of twenty-two. That's when the funds in your trust will revert entirely to you."

Out of nowhere, a thought popped up in the back of Chance's brain, and he was reminded of something he hadn't thought about for a long time—a wish he'd made to a comet when he was fifteen years old. A wish, legend said, that should be coming true about now, since Endicott had been celebrating the "Welcome Back, Bob" comet festival for a few weeks. Something cool and unpleasant wedged into his throat at the memory.

He eyed Poppy warily. "H-how much money is in that trust?"

Her serious green eyes had never looked more serious. "A million dollars, Mr. Foley. Once the children have reached the age of twenty-two, that million dollars will be yours."

Don't miss
Be Careful What You Wish For *by Elizabeth Bevarly,*
available August 2022 wherever
Harlequin Special Edition books and ebooks are sold.

Harlequin.com